All rights reserved. No reproduction, copy or transmissions of this publication may be made without written permission. No paragraph of this publication may be reproduced, copied or transmitted save with written permission or in accordance with the provisions of the Copyright Act 1956 (as amended). Any person who does any unauthorised act in relation to this publication may be liable to criminal prosecution and civil claims for damage.

Copyright © Sharon Plant 2023.

Telling Tales
Stories of Exmoor

Written by eleven members of
The Lynton Library Book Club

Telling Tales
is dedicated to
our dear friend
Nicky Ramsay
1953 - 2022

Never one to actively seek the lime-light Nicky would nevertheless be honoured and delighted to have had this book dedicated to her. She loved language and had a real passion and relish for the exploration and use of both the spoken and the written word. This was manifest in her eloquence as she brought stories to life, as she described her beloved plants while gently caressing their leaves, as she worked her way to the heart of the matter in her analysis of the elusive Samuel Beckett for her PhD. Her love of the exploration, meaning and function of words meant she really valued the Book Club as a place to regularly share and participate in the description and analysis of literature in its many forms. It really was an important part of her life on Exmoor.

And on her behalf, I thank you all.

Davy Ramsay, Jan 2023

Telling Tales

Written by eleven book lovers,
living on and around Exmoor.
Some fictional, some factual,
some autobiographical,
but all related to the moor.
The stories are presented in a
circular route starting from Lynton.

Any inaccuracies are the authors' own.

17. *Think Cow* by Marthe Kiley-Worthington
41. *Love Stories* by Sharon Plant
77. *Free Spirits* by Nicky Ramsay
107. *Hurlstone Point* by Graham Lavender
125. *Mayday* by Carolynn Gold
175. *The Swedish Girl* by Maria Floyd
189. *Mr Alexander* by Pat Young
215. *Walking Exmoor* by Angela Percival
233. *Brendon Common* by Helen Bolton
257. *A Man with Antlers* by Stephany Pettinger
275. *He Wanted to Try* by Anne King

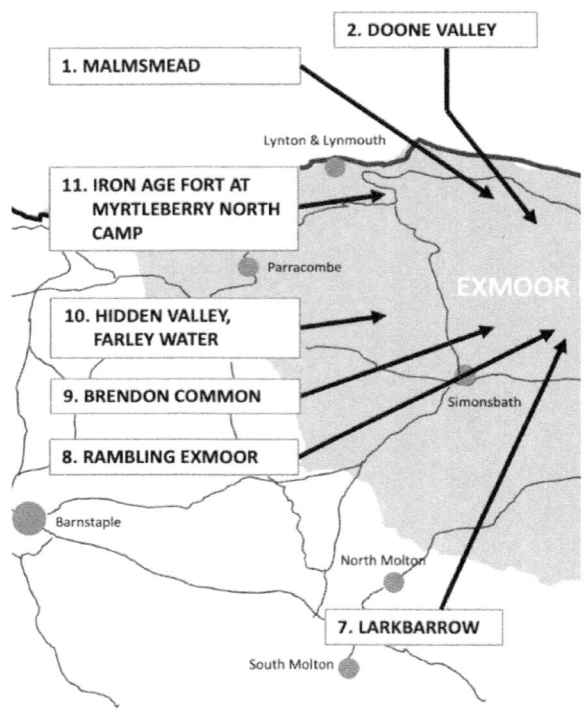

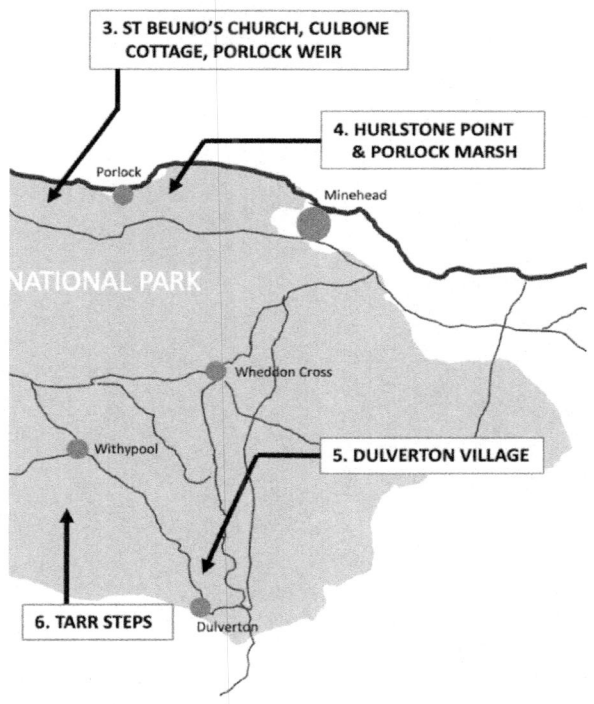

Telling Tales

An icy wraith slid across the Bristol Channel from the Brecon Beacons with one intent: to penetrate the crittall windows of her boot room. She crossed her arms and stared at Wales which, like the farm, was already under a layer of snow. She breathed in, breathed out, concentrating on the white puff of exhalation, ignoring the exasperation the windows provoked. Cold, hard, metallic, the frames inappropriate for the ancient farmhouse, the nature of which was surely to be warm, comforting, and homely.

A carrot cake wafted nutmeg and cinnamon into the kitchen, around the edge of which eleven chairs were set. The forecast was bad, more snow was expected this afternoon, but they had agreed to risk it; what was a little snow when they had heard the survival stories of the big freeze of 1962. Besides, they were ready. They had each spent the past three months composing a tale they hoped might capture something of the magic and mystery they had found on Exmoor. After they had discussed the monthly book, today was the day they were going to read aloud the first three tales. They had each brought their individual compositions, not knowing whose name might be drawn from the hat.

Car tyres dislodged the loose gravel of the drive, drawing lines in the snow.

She turned back to the kitchen to put on the kettle.

Graham bowled in through the door, his hands wedged hard into his armpits.

'Hello, hello, incoming. God it's good to reach some warmth.'

The door flew opened again.

'Only me, hello all. Oooo are we the first? Something smells good. I caught a ride with Graham. The drifts across from Porlock are stunning. We stopped to look at the ponies, locked in pairs, head to tail, such a neat solution, don't you think? Pragmatic, sociable, comforting; just what I might do if I were a pony.'

'Hello Nicky, come through, take a pew, wasn't sure if you would get across the moor today.'

'Wouldn't miss today for the world.'

The door opened and closed for ten minutes as members of Lynton Library Book Club ricocheted into the farmhouse boot room, wrapped in layers of scarves, hats, boots, all of which they shed to huddle in the candlelight of the kitchen.

The host knew candles the were not necessary, there being a perfectly adequate supply of electricity to light the room, but she felt at liberty to enjoy the strangeness of the weather and to indulge the group's pleasure of winter on Exmoor. If there had been a free-hanging pendant lamp, she might have set it swinging.

People exchanged greetings, hugs, news.

Teas were distributed, a peppermint here, a decaf there, and the room settled.

'We have had a few apologies,' she began, 'and sadly we are four members down this afternoon, but they are here in spirit, having sent their thoughts on the book.'

And, as is the nature of the meeting, conversation began in earnest, members offering responses to this month's title, some questioning the views of others, or the intentions of the author, some admitting they had found it challenging, others that they had loved it, and ordered more books by the author, and yet others that they had not got round to reading it, because work on the farm, visits from family, consultancy work of a professional nature, had robbed them of the time to properly enjoy it.

Cake was eaten, literary and personal anecdotes were shared, and as the afternoon wore on, the room was cast in the lilac light reflected by the snow; a fresh flurry of snowflakes began. They remarked on the fall, but it still seemed light enough, and they were keen to hear some of their own compositions. So, the names of the first three members were pulled from the hat and the writers began to read.

1

Think Cow

Marthe's Tale

7am, a typical Exmoor morning, overcast, slight drizzle now and then, and certainly a wind on the top of the hills as the trees' branches bounce about. We are in the Badgeworthy Valley, and moving all our farm, house equipment, and four-footed family across the moor to another farm which we hope will be real Exmoor and unlikely to be dominated by humans on their outings.... Today, after tractor and trailer have made about a dozen journeys around the lanes with junk, including trailer loads of manure to start our ecological farm and wildlife reserve, it is the migratory day for our horse stud, founded in 1959. We have three older mares, including Shemal the grand decision maker who runs the show and often us, our young future stallion, Larikyn who has already managed to "make love" to Shindi, (with her aid of course since horses can't rape each other unless they are tied up by humans... which they usually are.) The result: a cheeky adventure loving colt foal called Shebang. Shindi, is definitely someone who prefers motherhood and "house-keeping" to a profession, (although she was almost unbeaten when taking part in competitions). Shindi also has a two-year-old daughter, a filly Shakty who at one month old, came all the way from France in our multi-species van. Moto our oldest canine friend and worker and her rather scatterbrained son of five months Jo, are accompanying us. We saddle up, I ride Shatish, the son of Shemal and take his mother on a lead knowing that everyone else will then follow us, Chris, my partner is on the silver bullet Lilka, a feisty little person who will take anyone anywhere... if she likes.

The first part of the track is through abandoned Cloud Farm, the last chance to see this tumbled down Exmoor Farm before it is spruced up for "people viewing" by its new owners. We cross the river and continue up stream along the bank towards what is known as the "Medieval village", now a bunch of stones which, with some imagination, you can see might once have been houses. It was used for target practice in the last world war and succumbed to rubble; now covered in brambles and nettles; probably nicer than the stone cottages.

It is remarkably silent this morning, few birds singing, just the gurgle of the river where John Ridd of Lorna Doone fame caught fish... but now no fish live in the river due to run off of the many chemical applications on the banks and up stream. Over the last 50 years, the chemicals have probably penetrated to the water table feeding the springs. One of the causes of this, ironically, may be "conservationists" killing an invasive species, R*hododendron ponitum,* with poisons. Add to this, decades of chemical dipping and dosing of sheep against their pests and parasites, which kills all sorts of insects all over the moor. The sheep, known by some as "white maggots", swarm about us and through the forest. But maggots at least clean wounds. It is difficult to see what good too many sheep do to benefit themselves or anything else without large grant aids. One of the hidden effects of too many sheep, and money making for owners, is the reduction of species diversity on the moor, so that after a couple of centuries the "wet desert" appears to be the romantic wild reality of the moor, with fewer insects, and therefore fewer birds, fewer different species in the sward, no regeneration of woodland and therefore a destabilization of the living planet; an "ecological disaster cascade".

There is an old oak wood on the edge of the track, flaunting its many eco-niches in all its rotting trunks, hanging limbs and sprouting shoots, and a small area of bracken on a steep slope where there has been less sheep grazing. On this steep slope, unlike in the oak woodland, there are a few young trees: birch, blackthorn and willow poking their heads above the bracken and gorse who have acted as nurse crops for them. One wonders how long the oak forest will remain as it gently meanders down the steep slope north of the river because there are no young trees as they have not survived the attentions of the sheep in their first couple of years. But, there are a host of bilberries crowding along the path edge where there is enough light… strange to imagine the many peasants more than a century ago sitting singing in their pinafores and bonnets in these quiet gentle damp woods, collecting bilberries... not to eat but to sell for the blue dye they produce, one sometimes deeply envies them.

Exmoor is most famous botanically for its collection of bryophytes, the non-flowering wet loving plants, such as lichens, mosses, liverworts and hornworts. They cover every nook and cranny with their green or silver multi-shaped beings nuzzling on rocks, hanging from trees and painting the streams muddy banks with every shade of green and every shape of "leaf". One of the queer things about these ancient plants is that what we see is the generation which is equivalent in us mammals to that of the egg or the sperm, the "haploid" generation and their "diploid" generation (the one we see in all mammals) is a small, short often invisible little flat green mush. Lichens demonstrate how species can live together, in fact become dependent on each other. The lichens often blue/green/silver so commonly festooned from the little tree branches around Exmoor are the result of a symbiotic relationship between a fungus and an algae... they demonstrate mutualism, something that humans have often lost sight of... and they are particularly sensitive to air pollution so they do not flourish in large cities; demonstrating that one of the first species groups to die out due to human actions, are mutualistic ones: species living together with the rest of the living world ...not humans strong point at the moment!

Then there are the ferns, which like us are diploid, but go through a short generation that is haploid and must have water, even though the enormous glorious feathery leaves uncurling to wave their green selves in the wind can manage in relatively dry places, they cannot reproduce without their haploid prothallus generation. Nobody really knows why or how plants as they evolved changed from a predominantly haploid (like your sperm or egg) generation to a diploid one (where they fuse and double the chromosome numbers)... but there are a lot of deeply held beliefs. The irony is, it is widely also believed with considerable evidence, that after the living world holocaust the only living survivor will be those that are haploid and/or mutualistic.

We trundle on along the path, Shatish and Shemal pondering and watching the world but the foal gallops on ahead like youngsters of any mammal, then stops, stares, leaps away, snorts and finally blocking the path for the rest of us, so we all stop. The grown-ups, make the most of this by taking a quick snack of anything tempting within reach of their prehensile lips and furry muzzles; they know youngsters will do this as they explore the world because they know what youngsters know. Foals, unlike human babies and rats, are born at a late stage of development (precocial) and within hours they must learn to be able to get up, balance, walk, find a teat, recognise their mother and stay close to her. They have to learn how to work their bodies to balance and coordinate muscles to walk and canter, then, who their mother is and where the teat is. All this is learnt very fast after birth, if they survive. Compare this with the months it takes a baby to recognise a human face or direct its hand to clasp something, never mind to stand up and walk. As a result, calves and foals have enlarged forebrains, (the part of the brain that is mainly responsible for learning, decision making, and consciousness), when they are born and can have even more convolutions in the surface area of the cerebral cortex than humans. Once they have found the teat and recognise their mother, they then must set about learning about the environment they are in. That is, they must acquire a brainful of "ecological knowledge": where to find food, shade, water, what to eat and what not to eat, where to shelter if the wind is from the northeast and so on.

They also have to learn to become good sociologists ... learn who is who in their group, who to approach, who to avoid, who to follow, who knows what and who does not know. Although today there are few predators of large mammals around anywhere in Europe, nevertheless, they can still have accidents and make the wrong choices: drown in a river by following the wrong equine into it, break a leg by galloping too fast over difficult ground, or eat something that makes them ill by not watching what the knowledgeable group members eat.

As they grow up, they must continue to learn and the best way to do this is by being curious, but also careful of anything different or new. For example, if they have not seen water tumbling over a smooth large rock, a foal may stand transfixed for minutes. A beetle slowly making his way through the leaves of grass will be enough to cause a youngster to leap or snort, perhaps followed by a transfixed, intense stare. The older horses know, of course, that the youngsters are likely to react to everything as so much is new to them, so they often ignore their signs of "something scary about"... but should an older mare such as Shemal, the decision maker or even keep-apart-Lilka suddenly stop and stare, leap away or snort, then all will stop what they are doing, attend and stare in the same direction.

Thus, each adult horse in a group has learnt what another might know and also his or her personality, whether she is inclined to panic for no reason or remain calm, whether s/he is moody and bad tempered or affectionate, or just not very social. Each knows each other's role in the society. In this way, they learn who knows most and is best to follow in a particular different situation and who to ignore or who to avoid. But their society is not competitive, like that of hens and primates such as humans; their survival strength is their cooperation and tolerance of each other. This allows each to remain in the society and in this way by observing and imitating others, learn more about the world they live in and how to best survive and breed in it. Most of this knowledge is acquired from each other, called "social learning". The advantage of this, as we know from humans, is that each individual does not have to learn by trial and error, and the error can be very costly such as losing their life by not running away from a predator. By learning from each other, every individual does not have to "invent the wheel", he just has to use it, just like humans. But the practicality of learning to use it can also be difficult... we all learn "that" the wheel goes round and is helpful for transport, but we also need to learn the "how" to move the wretched thing...take for example riding a bicycle: anyone can see a bicycle and know that it is for riding... but he has to learn to ride it!

To live in society there must be a social contract, that is a bunch of rules which everyone learns and knows. Obeying these rules is sensible because if you do not, you stand a chance of being thrown out of the group. Such rules as "do not hurt a foal" or annoy a mare giving birth, or have sex with another stallion who is not of the group (at least if he can see you). Each individual knows when he has obeyed the rule or when he has not. For example, your dog knows when he has stolen the cake off the table and knows he has done wrong. Each individual knows the difference between right and wrong in that society; in other words, s/he is a "moral agent." Thus, equines, dogs (and all mammals at least) are not just the objects of moral concern by humans, which means that because they feel we must be nice to them, but they are also moral agents and know when they have done right or wrong according to the rules of that society whether this is one including different species or just their own. Moto, our collie, knows that she must not chase the sheep on the moor unless she is asked to... she would love to but must not on pain of getting rapidly told off... which she does not like at all, but also, the horses know they must not bite or kick a person or rush off when asked not to, because they have learnt that during their upbringing; it is part of the multi-species rules or social contract. Equally the humans in their group know that they must not constantly restrict and restrain them by hurting them, pulling at their mouths, tying their mouths up, or stopping them having a bit to eat when it does not matter. Like us, they must be able to make choices to do or not to do what we want, and we therefore must also ensure that they want to do what we ask, and we must become aware of what they are asking and why…. if we wish to live in a cooperative society.

As we wander up through the woods to the open moor above the medieval village, we all spot a small group of Exmoor ponies grazing, and watching us from around 100 meters. These guys have many of the same social rules as our horses have, but here and there they differ because they have had different experiences. It is as if they have learnt a different language. In effect, they come from a different culture… they have lived a different sort of life from our equines and us. In particular, they have had little direct contact with humans, although they see them often enough walking and biking around with their dogs, but they are rarely touched by them and know that humans on quad bikes who rush up behind them are frightening and they must move. They have also learnt from the older members of their community in which direction they need to move in order to stop being chased, which is why "the gather" of the ponies is so easy... they know which way they must go and it is only mistakes made by the quad bikers that cause them to go the wrong way! They in effect have a different culture from our horses and they have different knowledge of the environment and probably some slightly different social rules. But they can of course learn each other's rules, as our Exmoor pony Emma has, who stays close, even though she is loose and could quickly rush off to join a group of ponies on the moor if she wanted to. But she does not because although she was born on the moor and spent the first nine months of her life with her mother and her group, she has spent the last 18 months with us and learnt our multi species culture.

We know of course that just like another mammal, humans, different populations have different knowledge and different cultures... the only thing controlled by "instinct" is the need to learn, but what, where, when they learn depends on their lifetime experiences.

    We climb steeply through the oak wood and come out onto the open moor of Brendon Common where there still remains some heather interspersed with purple moor grass, a tufted grass that likes it wet. Gradually the view to the sea opens up in front of us. The moor is dotted with a few trees and bushes in the valleys where the sheep cannot or have not grazed, and further on towards the sea, all is enclosed into fields by walls, hedges and wire fences. These fields have been drained and reseeded sometime in the last century or two and grow often planted "improved" grasses, so they appear much brighter green. But there is one very distinctive character of the Exmoor hedges which divide them. On the tops of the walls that were originally constructed to keep stock in or out, beech trees were planted and some have grown into large trees. Many of these have remained untended for even a century, and have grown into big bold trees with their roots swirling about visibly in the walls beneath which are covered in mosses, ferns and liverworts.

    This was apparently the idea of Mr Knight who bought a large estate at Simonsbath in the 19th century. At the time, Simonsbath was a wind-swept isolated moorland farm and he planted the beech trees on top of the walls to improve the shelter for the grazing stock. The modern treatment is to annually chop and cut these trees which makes them easy to push through for the grazing ponies, cattle and sheep. Consequently, a wire and rylock netting fence has to be constructed around the old hedge thereby using masses of wire which as it is replaced or left becomes entangled in everything. It also loses the point of why the hedge was planted in the first place! To be fair, today there are generous grants available for farmers to "cut and lay" their hedges, which allows them to re-establish as a living stock barrier... in fact these are so generous that some farmers on Exmoor more or less live on the income the grant supplies! Ah well, there may be many roads to Rome, but we must be careful we don't end up in a nonliving desert by taking too many wrong turnings.

Knight was also influenced by the trend towards "natural" gardens fashionable at the time in Britain, so around his mansion, he re-constructed an exaggerated form of "nature" by moving large moss-covered boulders to be seen from the drawing room windows, or constructing fern glades by the small rivers, an early form of "re-wilding" of the garden.

In the enclosed paddocks on the edge of the moor there are still a few large old beech and oak trees probably as old as a century or more, isolated away from the canopy of others which allows them to spread their branches and obtain more light and beautiful gigantic shapes. They can live for centuries in this way and support a veritable world of little ecosystems in their wet crannies and corners, windy bits and dry faces. Branches die and decompose, and the great underground connecting mycorrhizal joins all the trees and other species together, the branches decompose and the great circle of life continues.

We wander over the moor towards our new home, the youngsters rushing here and there, or stopping to eat, then, left behind, panicking and galloping to catch up; the older horses determinedly marching towards the sea, and more grass, while taking in the views. We trot and then canter, gliding effortless over the rough pitted swampy or stony terrain with their four legs and extraordinary balance. Moto stays close to heel watching her manners and ensuring that no one strays too far from the group, while Jo has to be frequently reminded to stay with us and not lollop off following his nose on jaunts of his own. The sun even puts in a quick appearance as we come to the grand old beech on top of the wall of our new farm next to the tumbled down gate which denotes the boundary.

We descend slowly down the steep grassy field, scattering the trespassing sheep who have clambered through the neglected ring fence to feed on the delicious remains of ryegrass lays of some years. A couple of red deer hinds spot us from one of our neighbouring fields and melt away; I am hoping that they will become our frequent visitors.

We slip down towards another tumbled down gate, and below that, tin sheds in various forms of collapse appear before the enormous ugly barn rears its head from a mess of plastic, hardcore and rubbish carefully tipped to make a flat yard for silage. We all stand and stare, with horror in the eyes of all of us, but around the corner we come to a small brook bubbling by a patch of grass in which there is a young beautiful purple beach tree, a red rhododendron and a lilac tree who have just finished flowering. The horses begin to salivate at the sight of plenty of the green, green grass in the field the other side of the brook. Perhaps by giving nature a helping hand in one way or another, we can all feel at home here... the valley has no other houses, and plenty of old trees, the drive is long from the road, and the views from the top of the field are made for all of us to stare out to sea.

Shemal has a long history of making herself at home in many places from Dartmoor, all around France and now

Exmoor, and one can see her calculating the plusses and minuses of this new home and how to ensure that her group survives and prospers. Shatish has less experience and looks with interest all around him, although quickly astounded by flapping plastic and large echoing buildings. Larikyn takes his cue from his grandmother, Lilka who is independently investigate the nooks and crannies while tagging along behind, while the youngsters stand and stare with wonder at a new world full of potential for exploration.

Jo with his canine over developed sensitivity to smells believes he has been let loose in the canine equivalent of a large library and burrows about smelling and peeing and, finding a particularly delicious badger pooh, rolls and rolls in it, covering himself in such a strong smell of "another" that no one will ever recognise him, perhaps he thinks, who knows? While Moto watches everyone carefully, ensuring that they do not go further away from each other than she has decided they should.

Will we all make a go of it? Will we all enjoy it and genuinely feel at home? Will we all manage to re-construct it as we like, given our differences? Can we offer a pleasant life of quality to all our four-footed friends as well as ourselves, and if so, how? It is us humans who have brought all of us here, so although all will take part in how it evolves, we are the ones carrying the can, and we have a great deal to think about and to do to ensure that all our inhabitants, domestic and wild, have all their physical, emotional, social and intellectual needs fulfilled before we can truly say we have done it okay. This means that we must recognise that each species, as well as each individual of that species, will have their own take on this world at Cranscombe Cleave. Humans are one species, they are not superior, they have their own expertises, but they miss out on others. Perhaps the major challenge is to learn from each other something about others world views, needs and desires so that we can advance into the post-anthropocene age as all of us of different species learn how to live together and adapt to difficult conditions on this biological planet. In this way we may find that what we see as major problems become minor. We humans, perhaps, do not need so much "stuff", our needs and desires could then be more easily met, ... and our appreciation of being alive as part of the living world around us could be more fully enjoyed. We are one species among many, and each has their own expertise, their role, and their understanding of the world. Some of which may be so alien that we have to take a deep breath and remember what we have in common: "life", before trying to understand very different points of view. It is a hard task to really understand but, the different world views of different non-humans may well help us solve some of our planet's and personal problems.

One of my mantras is "think cow" when you are in a difficult situation... cows are the ultimate optimists, they may be up to their hocks in wet stinking muck, enclosed in ugly large buildings in large groups, unable to lie down or go anywhere, and they really do mind about this... but they recognise that at the side of the building the sun is shining and life goes on. Just in case you think they are stupid, in our tests for quick learning to perform new actions, the heifer learnt faster than the foal, puppy, guanaco or an elephant... so they are certainly not "stupid". The mantra "think cow" has often helped people in difficult situations, so try it and see how you fare.

Exmoor is a microcosm of the planet's biological problems but, give it a chance and it will demonstrate how it celebrates all life and so should we.

2

Love Stories

Sharon's Tale

Lily and Ray Riley had four children, and at the time of this story they were living in a narrow, terraced house in Stepney, London. They were doing well: Ray was down the Commercial Road Gas Works; Lily took in washing and ironing. But in the evening, as they listened to the radio, news from Europe grew more and more gloomy.

The year was 1938.

Talk down the market was making Lily anxious, she would like to get away from it all, just for a day or two, get some fresh air, calm her nerves. She didn't want to end up back in hospital.

She had squirrelled away a little money, earned from doing outwork for a toy maker, painting lead soldiers, disastrously, Ray liked to point out cheerfully to anyone who would listen. She was ready to raise the subject.

Casual as you like, she suggested the possibility of her and Ray taking a short holiday.

'Get away by ourselves,' she knew how to get his attention. 'Maybe get Charlie and Connie to mind the kids.'

Ray tapped loose pipe ash into the ashtray balanced on the arm of his chair, took his pipe scraper from his top pocket and scratched it slowly around the bowl of the pipe.

Ray's brother Charlie, sitting as usual in the chair beside the fire, looked up from Ray's newspaper. 'Sounds a grand idea, Lil. Connie 'n' me can help out. No sense having us in-laws living in your back room if you can't make use of us. We'd be pleased to watch the kids.'

'Nothing expensive mind, perhaps cheap lodgings, or a spare room in a farm, maybe,' she added, appearing to talk to Charlie while keeping a sideways eye on Ray. 'Nowhere too busy, away from the crowds, and just for a weekend, perhaps over the August Bank Holiday.'

'And where might this 'ere 'oliday take place?' asked Ray, careful not to look directly at Lily.

Lily had read a book.

A novel.

A novel for the seventeenth century.

She had slipped into the library as often as she could on her way back from the market and was now truly taken with the notion of seeing Exmoor.

'Exmoor,' she said.

'Exmoor!' cried Ray. 'Where the heck's that! I'll bet its blooming miles from anywhere.'

'Exactly, it's miles from anywhere,' said Lily calmly. 'There's this farm that I'd like to see, Malmsmead Farm it's called, near a ford, in the Doone Valley.'

'The Doone Valley? Never heard of it,' said Ray. 'I can always take you down the River Lee.'

'It's dangerous and wild and romantic.'

'So's the River Lee.'

'In this book there's gangs, robbery, violence.'

'We can get that in Clacton.'

'And the hero's father gets murdered.'

'Southend then,' said Ray.

'By Carver Doone, the leader of the gang. And John Ridd, the hero, travels to London to visit the King.'

'Lil, we've no need to go to the back of beyond to find out why some Ridd fella came to where we are already.'

'And would you believe the luck of it! After a talk with Mary at the exchange, and Mary then talking to her sister-in-law's cousin who lives down that way, a very nice woman came back to the cousin to say that she was the current owner of Malmsmead Farm and that she had a room available. And we've exchanged a few letters since, and I've explained my interest and she says the room's not much like, but still. And it's only a florin for the two nights.'

'How much?' barked Ray. 'Don't be crazy, Lil! And it'll cost an arm 'n' a leg to get there! You'd have to paint a battalion to earn that sort of money!' He chortled to himself.

'So I said yes, we'd take it.'

Ray lowered his pipe and stared at his wife.

No Clacton, no Southend, no by your leave.

Charlie smiled.

*

Ray had the hump.

First the walk to the bus depot, then the long, parched wait on the long, parched railway platform, followed by the slowest train ever to pull out west of London, then a train change, until finally they ended up in some outback place called Minehead, from where they had to take another flaming bus. I ask you, and all the time him lugging the suitcase.

Eventually, the bus set them down nicely, the driver pointing to a road heading steeply downhill signposted to Oare Church.

Ray looked unconvinced.

Lily looked pleased as punch.

Off she marched down the hill.

'I have it clear as can be in my mind, Ray,' she called back, Ray followed grudgingly behind. 'I'm looking to find the spot where the book said John Ridd discovered the hidden route into Doone territory, climbed a water slide, slept with the exhaustion of it all, then woke to find himself being minded by Lorna.'

Ray felt some sympathy for this exhausted John Ridd. But he knew how Lily got when one of them library books took her fancy, all wound up and over the top, and usually he was not of a mind to complain, in fact, he enjoyed hearing her stories, but this whole Exmoor malarky was pushing it a bit. 'Not too sure what you're on about, Lil. You're gonna have to explain this book again.'

'Lorna Doone, Ray, I did say. John Ridd didn't even know who she was when he first saw her.'

Ray shifted the suitcase from one hand to the other, trudging along reluctantly, making a definite point of dragging his feet.

And exhaling loudly.

He stared at Lily's back.

Then he stopped, put down the suitcase, sat on it with a grunt and gestured to Lily to sit beside him. He was hot, tired, and not a little grumpy. He flicked at a purple thistle.

'So, we've traipsed all this way, to look for a made-up waterfall, in a made-up valley?'

'And also, to see the church where Lorna Doone was shot.'

'And to look for a made-up church because a made-up bloke was interested in this treacle.'

'Well, it's not all made up, Ray. The church is real.'

She paused.

'And, besides, John Ridd spoke to me.'

Ray looked at her, his eyebrows lifting to his fringe. 'Uhuh. You're saying this bloke in this book spoke to you.'

'When I was in the library one time, reading the book, I leant back in the chair, closed my eyes to picture the scene, and John Ridd's voice spoke to me. He said something about how mad the Doones made him. How they'd murdered his father while he were a lad. Embarrassed his uncle, made him ride backward on an Exmoor pony. But what got him hoppin' was when he'd heard they were forcing Lorna to marry Carver Doone.'

'John Ridd spoke to you, did he? And he said all that? You didn't perhaps just doze off, Lil?'

'He did indeed. And she's not just any old treacle, Ray, she's the sweetheart in a very special love story. This is Richard Doddridge Blackmore's Lorna Doone.'

'Doddridge,' Ray repeated, a small grin starting to form. He studied his shoes, one of which was smeared with a healthy smudge of sheep poo. He took a large hanky from his pocket and made a drama of wiping his forehead. Then used it to wipe his shoe.

Lily ignored him, stood, and continued down the path.

Ray stood and followed. Why they were on this fool's errand in a sticky, clammy August he had no idea. 'And why would this particular guy, from this particular book, think to talk to you?' he called.

'Well, according to the story, he'd been to see the witch Ma Melldrum, who spends half the year in a shack in some place called the Valley of the Rocks, and the other half in a cave at a place called Tarr Steps.'

'She sounds a barrel of laughs.'

'And Ma Melldrum had advised John Ridd to have nothing to do with any Doone.'

'Ha! Finally! Someone with a lick of sense. But, again, why did he choose to talk to you, down the local library? Not really his manor, is it. This made-up guy surely has better things to do with his time.'

'Oooo Ray look, we must be almost there, there's the ford, and I'm guessing that must be the farm, just as the bus driver said.'

Ray perked up immediately. 'Not a moment too soon, Lilian. Let's see if there's a brew on the go.' With which he hoisted the suddenly lightweight suitcase onto his shoulder and strode off towards the farm.

After some bustle and handshaking and introductions and a lot of smiling they were shown up a narrow staircase, the ample rear of Mrs Richards preceding them, into a small room. Ray squeezed in behind Lily, thought about the florin, thought about a broom cupboard, thought about the swinging of cats, and was about to share his thoughts when Lily caught his eye.

He was silent.

As soon as they'd used the facilities and what not, which were out back and across the yard, Mrs Richards, the farmer's wife, said she would have the kettle on the stove ready to tell them everything they wanted to know about the farm, and of course, any more that she could tell Lily about the Doones, that she might have left out of her letters.

Ray did what he thought might be a fair impression of looking eager to hear more, followed by a grin to Lily.

Mrs Richards busied herself around her kitchen as Lily repeated some of their exchanges for Ray's benefit.
'And Mrs Richards' father was the Churchwarden at Oare Church, and the Ridds and their kin are still living hereabouts!' said Lily, wide eyed with enthusiasm.
Ray dunked a biscuit into the steaming tea.
'And you play the organ, don't you Mrs Richards?' Lily continued, barely able to contain her awe.
'That's right, Mrs Riley, that I do. I bin playin' the organ 'ere since I can't remember when.' Mrs Richards burst into fabulous laughter at this thought. ''N' I can tell you this for nuthin, Mrs Riley: I am never grown tired o' talkin' 'bout Lorna Doone. She's like a chil' o' me own.'
Lily nodded her appreciation. 'And is the church as it was in the novel?'
'Gor no, m'dear. There's bin all sorts o' change since then. For a start, there'd be no glass in place.'

'How'd they see out then?' quipped Ray.

Lily gave him a look.

'In the time o' the Doones, the church would 'ave ended where the screen is now, 'n' the window in the south wall, well, that would 'ave been open to the elements.'

Ray nodded to imply this might be an interesting piece of information, to someone, and picked up another biscuit, wondering if there was any more tea in the pot.

''N' the box pews, well they were not yet in the nave, they would 'ave been open benches, like those what you see up at Culbone.'

Lily didn't know what this meant but she loved all the unfamiliar words, she loved this woman's pleasure, and she loved Mrs Richards for making it sound so thrilling.

''N' when you goes to the church, mind you look west o' the door. There's a memorial plaque bin put there, put up about ten year ago, to Richard Doddridge Blackmore.' Mrs Richards smiled broadly, as if she were in some way responsible for its erection. 'There's talk that it's a copy of one in Exeter Cathedral, not that I've seen that mind, but still, Exeter Cathedral, no less.' She ran her finger down the braided edge of her pinny. 'Exeter Cathedral,' she nodded.

Ray bit his lip, swallowing another ill-judged quip.

'We'll be sure to look for it, Mrs Richards,' said Lily.

'But somethin' you might not know, Mrs Riley, is that Blackmore's own grandfather were Rector at Oare! Though between you 'n' me, he were scant seen, according to parish records, but still. Who knows, maybe it's that what made the grandson think to set his big scene in the church!'

'Yes, maybe!'

Ray looked up. 'Aren't you going to tell Mrs Richards about your conversation with John Ridd, Lil? The one in the library,' he prompted.

Lily silenced him with a stare. Ray examined the tea leaves in his cup. 'Seems a shame not to,' he began...

'Now, yous twos 'ave been on the road since sun up so you might be expectin' some tea around now. I've a new loaf, 'n' some o' me own cheese. N' this year's tomatoes what are just about perfect, and some o' me rhubarb chutney.'

'Sounds lovely, Mrs Richards,' said Lily eagerly.

Ray beamed. Yep, fine by me.

Mrs Richards plumped around the kitchen piling things onto the table: chipped crockery, bent knives, a milk jug without its handle, a slab of yellow butter, a crusty loaf, half a truckle of cheese, a bowl of pink chutney, some large, polished tomatoes, a cracked bowl of boiled beetroot.

Spotting the covered plate warming on a saucepan, Ray asked, 'Mr Richards working late this evening then?'

'Aye, that 'e is. It's a busy time. The shearin's sorted, but e'll be startin' up at the Telling House shortly for the brandin'. Hisself and the dogs'll round up the sheep for countin'.'

'He'll sleep well at night then,' remarked Ray, looking up at her face for an amused response.

'That he will,' responded Mrs Richards, pokerfaced, 'providing the tally is as we's expectin' and none o' them 'ave bin stoled.'

'Stolen,' said Lily. 'Does that happen, Mrs Richards?'

'I'll say it does! Can't trust these buggers round 'ere as far as you can throw 'em. But when the rams is in, that's when you needs eyes in the back of your 'ead. They's mighty valuable a good ram is, an' your own neighbour is as likely to filch 'im to service his own fields as any other tom, dick or harry.'

'Descendants of the Doones, perhaps,' suggested Ray, recalling their roguish skulduggery as described by Lily.

'Oh aye, some o' them for sure are.'

Mrs Richards refilled the battered kettle and put it back to boil.

Ray was ready for a refill. 'Do you get to London ever, Mrs Richards? Maybe for some window shopping?'

Mrs Richards looked at Ray for a moment. It was clear from her expression that Mrs Richards was considering what window shopping might be. 'What'd I be doin' that for?' she asked, puzzled. 'B'ain't no call for me to go to London.'

'But you've been to Exeter, or Bristol, say?'

'I got all I needs right 'ere on this farm,' she said, with a hint of pique.

Lordy, thought Ray. 'So you have spent a full and jolly life on this 'ere moor?'

'Yes'm, I should say I 'ave?' she said with pride. 'And as for this 'ere window shoppin' you's talkin' of, that sure sounds like a fine waste o' time.'

'True, true, I suppose, as you seem to have all the windows you might reasonably need,' said Ray. 'But Lil says even John Ridd took himself off to London, for a spell.'

'That he did, Mrs Riley's not wrong there, but *he* were summoned, by the king hisself, James II that is, so's he'd no choice in the matter.'

It's possible we'll all be summoned by the king hisself in the not too distant future, thought Ray, from what he'd heard on the wireless. But he kept the thought to himself. Now that he'd recovered from the journey, he was starting to enjoy this idea of Lil's to get away for a break. Something out of the ordinary to tell the lads down the works.

The next morning, Lily was up and ready to walk Doone Valley before the sun had even warmed the path.

Ray was up and ready to enjoy Mrs Richards' hearty breakfast, which was wafting up the farmhouse stairs to the broom cupboard in which he'd spent a surprisingly comfortable night.

He would have lingered longer in the yeasty warmth of the kitchen but for Mrs Richards, who had packed them a lunch sack and was keen to get on with her day's work. She shuffled them out with instructions to keep to the right of the river and take the right fork before the old bridge then follow the trail to climb the hill up onto the moor.

'There's rain on the way so yous'll probably get wet. And there's some bachelors up there that'll be keeping an eye on you. Don't get too close, they can be a bit short-tempered.'

Ray had no idea what she meant, but it sounded bad.

They set off on the track described, beside a wide stretch of river that spilt into the fields, sloshing along in the oversized boots borrowed from Mrs Richards, after much tut tutting at their London footwear.

Ray kept pace, pondering the idea that he really was a city fella, one who enjoyed the hard flagstones under his feet, the echo of his footsteps on the terrace walls, the raising of a hand to hail the familiar face of a neighbour, the interrogatory look he reserved for anyone on his manor that he did not recognise, who was probably up to no good. He loved feeling packed in together, being part of the crowd, the hubbub in the cafe, the jostle in the chippy, knowing Charlie would be ambling in after a day's gardening duties and that Lily and Connie would be giggling in the kitchen in their cramped little terrace. Just the eight of them. He loved it. What was there to see or do in the country? It was... absolutely empty.

'Isn't the country lovely, Ray?' said Lily.

'Absolutely,' said Ray.

They picked their way between mud slurries, and what Ray assumed was elephant excrement.

Lily was thrilled. 'Imagine being able to write a whole book about a place like this, get it all down on paper in your own clever words, so that other people can see your waterfalls and valleys, so that people can almost smell your air, and know that this valley doesn't smell like chip fat, and the trees aren't dripping with pea soup smog. I think I can even smell the river! Is it possible to smell water?'

Ray inhaled. Could he smell the river? He wasn't sure. It was probably that elephant poo. But Lily was a marvel to him: the things she thought about!

'You'd better tell me this story then Lil; what are we actually here to see?' he asked with a resigned sigh. 'What was in this book that we have traipsed the width of the country to look at?'

'Well,' said Lily, delighted, 'as I said, it's a love story, with more than the usual twists and turns, and also it's a history book. The Doones lost their Scottish land and moved to Exmoor to live in hiding, where for thirty years or so they terrorised everyone who is not of their clan.'

'Sounds like the Hoxton Mob!'

'Charles II has died, his brother has taken the throne, but he is challenged by the old king's illegitimate son, who is eventually made king in a town near here, somewhere called Bridgwater.

'And it's a funny book, Ray. For instance, there's a man called Tom Faggus, who is John Ridd's cousin. He is a highwayman, but also a blacksmith, and he makes round horseshoes for his horse Winnie, isn't that a good name for a horse, Ray? And they're made round so as when he's out riding Winnie in these horseshoes, the law can't tell which way Tom's heading.'

'Are round horseshoes still lucky?' broached Ray.

'And Lorna, who has a mysterious start, washed ashore in a shipwreck, is betrothed, against her wishes, to a nasty piece of work, and John Ridd has to save her from a house where they're holding her prisoner, where she's been locked up so she won't run away from the marriage, and he and Lorna have this special code where Lorna's maid climbs into a tree, and when she puts six rooks' nests in the tree, Lorna is in trouble, but if there's only five nests, then she has been carried off by the Doones.'

'Bit of a palaver, don't you think. Why not just one or two nests?'

Lily stopped to inspect a fern, running her fingers through the fronds: tough yet delicate, wiry yet soft, thin upright leaves standing perkily to attention. She would take a strand home for the kids. Ray watched; his hands deep in his pockets. She continued walking.

'But the leader of the clan, Sir Ensor, is dying, and Lorna and John Ridd go to him on his deathbed to ask if they can marry, which at first he won't allow, but then he gives in, and tells them that in fact, Lorna is an important lady, an heiress to a fortune.'

'Aha! I thought so! No one would bother making up such a yarn if they'd been poor folk.'

'You don't think?'

'So the book is called Lorna Doone, and she isn't even a Doone!' he said triumphantly, as if in some way vindicated.

'I know!' she said, although in fact, this had not actually occurred to her.

She bent to inspect a small, yellow plant with pairs of two-lipped flowers sprouting up one side of the stem. Little kisses, she thought. She stood and continued along the path.

'But then, when they go to Oare Church to get married...oh...is this the path,

Ray, where we are meant to turn right? Up there is the bridge, here might be where Mrs Richards said we should climb up onto the moor.'

Ray looked suspiciously at the overgrown footpath. 'To meet the aggressive bachelors,' he said warily, eyeing the horizon. Must be the local troublemakers, he thought.

'Indeed,' said Lily, starting up the hill.

This was some climb.

The summit was further away each time he looked.

Ray had decided he should bring up the rear, but he was fading fast.

And there was still some way to go.

He knew he should have brought his pipe.

It would have helped with his breathing.

Good Lord, why are we doing this, he heaved, muttering to himself.

'Aw Ray, look at the colours of the heather, just starting to turn to Autumn. Orange, yellow, purple, with their tiny little egg-shape flowers, nothing like the dead grey sprigs the gypsy hands out on the corner.'

'Nothing like,' agreed Ray between gasps.

After what must have been about a week, Ray thought, Lily was at the top, climbing a gate, her hand shielding her eyes, scanning the view.

'It's so wild,' she cried, the wind dragging her voice away. 'It goes on for ev....!'

Ray reached the gate.

Leant casually on the top bar.

Lily wasn't even panting.

'Perhaps now's a good time to check out the lunch sack?' Ray said.

'This must be the way. Mrs Richards said keep to the wall until we get to the third gate, then we'd a choice. Either we should follow one of the tracks across the moor, or we could go down what she called a scree and retrace our steps along the river.'

'Which is shortest?' asked Ray, struggling over the gate.

Lily looked at him. 'You okay? You've gone a bit white.'

He made a show of taking in the view. The longer he pretended to admire the emptiness, the more he felt able to breathe. So where are these bachelors I'm to look out for, he thought?

'Maybe we could sit here against this wall and eat something,' she said.

*

Ray scrunched up the empty lunch sack and pushed it into his jacket pocket. They rejoined the path and walked on.

'Very nice,' he said, recovered, and stepping off the path onto the heather.

A loud shriek.

Out of the ground leapt a wild screech that made his hair bristle, something large, decidedly dangerous, certainly alien, squawked and screamed at him.

Ray shielded his head, threw himself to the ground, just in time for the pheasant to clatter into the air and glide over the wall.

But Ray knew, he had felt the dagger immediately, the bachelors must have crept up behind him, and one of them was holding a knife to his neck. One of the Southend Mob, doubtless.

He yelled, grabbed at his neck and felt the sharp bone jutting up out of the heather.

He panicked.

Not my bone surely, he thought, running his finger around the inside of his collar.

Lily saw the same. 'Why, I think you might have found an antler!' she said, pulling it out of the heather. 'Won't the kids be pleased!'

Ray looked at the offending antler.

Indeed, he thought, massaging his neck. Won't they just.

Ray was more than relieved when the farm came into sight.

Mrs Richards waved them in to another fine brew.

Over a strong cuppa, they shared their antler story, and she showed them the antlers her husband had brought in from around the farm.

'They're cast off, one at a time you know, but sometimes, when you's lucky, you gets to find the pair. They shed around May, and new ones starts growing straight away, each year bigger than the year before. Splendid things aren't they,' she said. 'Little miracles, really.'

'Miracles,' chimed Ray.

'And you're likely to find plenty on Exmoor as I've heard the red deer have been here since pre-historic time. And this, once being a Royal Forest, well, the king would have been keen to maintain his venison supply wouldn't he!' said Mrs Richards, with a hearty peel of laughter.

'Thanks for the tea, Mrs Richards. We're going to walk up to the church now.'

'We are?' said Ray. 'I thought it might be nice to sit out in the late sun for a bit.'

'Well you can, if you want. I don't mind walking up there on my own. It's a lovely evening.'

'Right-e-o,' he said. 'Don't get lost. And don't talk to any strangers, especially them bachelors.'

Lily picked up the clunky boots and started to put them on. 'I've a mind to walk through the ford, just to feel how cold the water is.'

'Don't be daft, Lil, you'll catch your death.'

'Do you think? Okay, I'll just feel it with my hand. The water's nearly four inches deep: it wouldn't do to get washed away.'

Ray looked at her; was she being funny?

Lily sat down on the bank of the river and unlaced the boots. She dipped her fingers in the river. It was cold.

It must have been difficult for you, John Ridd, she thought, knowing your Lorna was held prisoner, with the snow so deep you could not get through.

'It was a shocking winter that year. They called it *The Great Winter*.'

Lily spun round.

A man dressed in a loose linen shirt, a leather doublet, knee-length breeches, and a wide brimmed hat stood behind her.

Startled by his attire, by his sudden presence, by her distance from the farm, she jumped up, clutching the boots to her chest for protection.

The man smiled.

'But it all came well,' he said, 'in time. I remembered seeing the Doones returning from the ambush with a child across their saddle. And I came to understand that the glass necklace Lorna wore, was no trinket at all, was not glass as was supposed, but was in fact a valuable heirloom, and the clue to her past.'

Lily looked from side to side. What was going on? In the library he had simply spoken, but here, here he was!

'But Blackmore, our writer, he had insight, so much so that he could paint this woman of wealth and standing, as someone who knew that the only thing of real value, was love.'

Lily looked towards the farm. Where was Ray? He was supposed to be sitting out in the sun, where he might have seen her. Ah, there he was.

'Ray, Ray,' she called.

Ray looked up, waved, and settled himself back on the grass to read a week-old newspaper.

When she looked back, the stranger was gone.

Lily pushed her feet back into the boots and walked quickly over the bridge.

Sparrows and chaffinch hopped in and out of the hedgerows, rustling and busy. A wren bobbed. A blackbird squatted in the dust with its wings spread wide, soaking in the sun, undisturbed by her passing. A robin accompanied her, dipping up and down on its matchstick legs, flying on a few feet, then dipping again.

    She was unsettled.
    Turning the bend, she had her first glimpse of St Mary's Church at Oare, the very one in which Lorna Doone had been shot by Carver; she walked faster towards it, seeking refuge.
    Running up the steps, her heart beating, she stood for a moment in the small porch to steady her breath, reading the church notices. Had she really seen him?
    Please come in, said a sign on the door, *closing the door behind you, as birds entering become disoriented and flustered if they become trapped.*
    That would not have been a problem in Lorna Doone's time she thought, when presumably they came in through the glassless windows for shelter.

    The cool atmosphere was calming.
    She stood for a minute to steady herself.

Her footsteps echoed as she walked around the entranceway.

She paused before the organ pipes, marvelling at Mrs Richards' ability to draw tunes from such a daunting machine.

She ran her hands along the small doors of the box pews, smelling the lilac wax she imagined being applied by diligent parish custodians.

She found the memorial plaque to Richard Doddridge Blackmore, as Mrs Richards had described, to the left of the door. Such a kindly face, she thought, with its nearly smile. Carved in the stone beneath his portrait she read:

"INSIGHT, AND HUMOUR, AND THE RHYTHMIC ROLL OF ANTIQUE LORE, HIS FERTILE FANCIES SWAY'D, AND WITH THEIR VARIOUS ELOQUENCE ARRAY'D HIS STERLING ENGLISH PURE AND CLEAN AND WHOLE."

"HE ADDED CHRISTIAN COURTESY, AND THE HUMILITY OF ALL THOUGHTFUL MINDS, TO A CERTAIN GRAND AND GLORIOUS GIFT OF RADIATING HUMANITY."

Ray's head appeared around the church door.

Lily jumped.

'Ooo it's you,' said Lily, more than pleased to see him. 'Come through. Isn't it pretty?'

Ray stepped quickly inside, closing the door as instructed by the notice.

He always felt intimidated, apprehensive even, in a church, as if he might have done something wrong.

He went and stood close to Lily.

'It says here there was a John Ridd as Churchwarden between 1914 and 1925, isn't that exciting?'

'It is that,' said Ray, looking up at the wagon roof, with its sweeping ribs and bosses. 'Look at the angle on that wood, Lil, whoever carved that knew what they were up against.'

They walked up the nave, Lily reading the walls, Ray admiring the workmanship.

He stopped at a wooden message exhorting him not to covet his neighbour's house, nor his wife, nor servant, nor maid nor his ars.

Ray grinned, and turned to point out this interesting script, but looking at Lily thought better of it.

Lily had settled herself in the first pew.

'So,' said Ray, sliding in beside her, 'how did it all end? This Doone stuff. Happily I'll hope?'

Lily studied the eagle carved pulpit.

'Well,' she said. 'Lorna, it turns out, is nobility, one Lady Dugal, so she is taken to London under the guardianship of an uncle, and unknown to her, her maid does not forward her letters to John Ridd, because she believes a farmer is too low for a Lady, so they are parted. But eventually, John Ridd's sister marries Tom the highwayman, then Lorna comes of age, rejoins Ridd, farmers burn down the Doone village, although Carver escapes, and all seems about to end happily, here in this church, with John and Lorna's wedding, when Carver Doone shoots her dead.'

'The blaggard!' says Ray, jokily.

'John Ridd, angry, chases Carver into Black Bog.'

'I should think so too! You would, wouldn't you. Especially it being your wedding day. Good on Ridd.'

'And Carver is sucked into the bog.'

'I knew it was dangerous up there!'

'And that's the end of him.'

'Good *ridd*ance to him! Did you see what I did there, Lil? *Ridd*ance.'

'But now Ridd too is ill.'

'There's not much of a happy ending here is there, Lil. It's all a bit gloomy.'

'Well no, because Lorna is not dead, just at death's door.'

'So she lives and now he dies?'

'No, it's a proper fairy tale ending, everyone survives, and they all live happily ever after.'

'Aww, well, that's nice.'

'And John and Lorna, well, they're a bit like us, don't you think, Ray?'

'How do you mean?'

'Well, we've had our troubles, haven't we? You took me to hospital when I could have died from those burns.'

'But you didn't.'

'And then we nearly lost Charlie.'

'That was bad, but it's righted now.' Lily smiled.

'But you're right, Lil, it's a great story.'

'It's a great love story,' corrected Lily.

'With John and Lorna having lots of troubles but ending up happy as Larry.'

'Indeed.'

'Like us,' said Ray.

'Yes.'

'I guess you could say, they ended up living the life of Riley,' said Ray, with a boyish celebratory punch at the air. Lily rewarded him with a smile.

It's a funny thing, life, thought Ray, as, hand in hand, they walked back to the farm. Some people claim they can talk with the dead, but my wife, my Lil, she goes one further and chats with the made-up dead. That takes the biscuit.
It also made him feel strangely proud.

The bus bounced along a windswept road weaving its way back to Minehead and the train station: Lily had had a marvellous time. The antler was carefully nestled in the suitcase, waiting for its big ta-dah when they got to Stepney, along with a fern frond, and a sizeable wedge of Mrs Richards' cheese, which she had assured them was far better than any they could get in the city. How would she know, thought Ray, mystified by her certainty. More likely, all it would do was make his clothes smell high.
Lily squeezed his hand three times, their code for *I love you*.

Ray squeezed her hand in return, his face a ruddy glow. 'So, what was your favourite bit?' he asked.

She looked out the window and smiled. 'Meeting John Ridd.'

3

Free Spirits

Nicky's Tale

The first thing Sophie realised as she pounded up the twisty vertiginous path towards Culbone church was that her Doc Marten boots felt too heavy, too hot and too altogether set on beating out her own fury to be entirely comfortable. Her mission to reach Culbone was probably a perverse one in the first place, as she had reacted badly to the suggestion of a family walk earlier that morning. They had all set out, mum, dad, and younger brother but when her mother had complained of a dodgy ankle and started to limp, the whole thing had been called off. "Come back, Sophie, Mum's not up to it. We'll try again another time" Dad had texted, but Sophie, striding ahead as usual, was having none of that! They had forced her out on this stupid walk in the first place, and she was b***** well going to show them that she, Sophie would do it, come what may. She glanced back furtively and realised that they had indeed gone, the path behind was undeniably unpeopled. She allowed herself to feel a tiny bit of sadness as she realised that her family had not tried particularly hard to get her to return with them.

As soon as sure she was truly on her own, she allowed herself to slow the pace and realised that she had never before actually been on a country walk by herself. She had a strange impulse, first of panic, then of exhilaration as her breath eventually began to slow down and the urgent tempo of her walking steadied. Things had not been going so well for her of late. She would be leaving home soon to take up her place at uni and having resolutely refused the notion of a gap year as a complete waste of time, the future seemed immense, and a little dreadful. The whole prospect made her feel giddy in spite of her furious manner and insistent statements that she needed to break free. Be that as it may, here she was now, striding out on her own in the very last environment that she would willingly have chosen. In the past, the very thought of 'Nature' had brought on a fit of the horrors! Somehow now though, with every pace, she was finding anger a little more difficult to muster. The trees, which at the start had mainly been recognisable native trees, now gave way to a series of deep green Corsican pines. These with their magnificent outlines stirred rather pleasant memories of an Italian holiday the family had once had in the deep past, during calmer times. As she turned bend after bend she found she looked forward to the moments when the skyline allowed her to catch glimpses of an intensely blue sea. She knew that the ascent would take a while. She had been told that it was about two miles, mainly uphill all the way. The rest of the family had special devices on their phones and Fitbits to tell them how they were doing, but she began to rather like the idea of just putting one foot in front of the other and allowing her sense of youthful vigour to carry her onwards and upwards. After all, she was very good at swimming, it was the only real physical activity she ever did these days. In swimming she could both lose herself and have a curious sense of finding herself at the same time.

    Suddenly, a little ahead of her on the track, a small collarless dog comes into sight. Sophie immediately braces herself to confront the inevitable owners who would follow it and she gets out her habitual stony non-communicative face. But oddly, no-one comes and instead of continuing on down the hill behind her, the little dog has now turned around and seems to want to stick by her side. He seems completely at ease, not a lost dog, just one who has a firm sense of himself and is clearly self-directed! She starts to play some tricks with this scruffy little chap and finds that if she goes along slowly, he does too and likewise if she speeds up, he would race to catch her up. They were both having a lot of fun with this game and she had by now almost forgotten about the destination, when all at one, round one final bend, the tiny church of Culbone comes into view.

By now Sophie is sweating heavily. Long ago she has taken off her leather jacket and tried to tie it round her waist, awkwardly. But she herself is now feeling anything but awkward. She is full of a sense of triumph. She has made it here, after all. But more than anything now her desire is to find some water. Maybe there is a tap on one of the church walls, the sort that flower arrangers use to fill their vases and pitchers? She flings down the jacket, grateful to be released from its weight and starts to make a circuit of the old stone walls. As she turns around an angle of the church, she notices a small oddly shaped window with a chink open to the elements. She remembers talk at the supper table last night of how a 'leper chink' in the walls of Culbone church allowed the local leper colony a glimpse of what was going on inside the church while effectively excluding them. Last night, this had made her very angry and she had had an uncontrollable outburst at the injustice of this. Looking now, all she can feel is a tender sense of pity for the wretches outside who were desperately trying to find a little comfort by getting as close as they could, perhaps clambering up in turns to get a glimpse of the comfort and humanity within.

    Thinking these thoughts, Sophie is once again aware of her own urgent need for a drink and she continues to look for the tap. Gleefully, she finds what she is looking for. It looks a bit rusty and there's not much of a flow but all at once she knows what she must do, and abandoning the tap she runs to follow the sound of the stream that runs alongside the church. Why hadn't she thought of this before? She can hear her mother's prohibition, warning against falling in and the likelihood of a dead sheep upstream. But she knows what she wants and ripping off the offending hot chafing boots, Sophie splashes into the small stream. Feeling an unusual sense of freedom as her sweltering feet respond gratefully to the ice-cold eddies of water, she bends to scoop up thirst quenching palmfuls of delectable spring water. At first it all drains through her fingers, after all she's never done this before, but she finally gets the hang of it and takes in long deep gulps. At last she leaves the water, and is suddenly compelled by a sense of indescribable fatigue, overcome by the arduous climb and the nervous energy which has propelled her up here to this lonely place. Making a pillow of her leather jacket, she settles down onto a grassy bank and closes her eyes, just as Ruggles comes out of the water and shakes himself vigorously. This makes Sophie laugh as she is sprayed yet again. Then stretching out contentedly, she allows herself to fall back into a deep slumber with the little scrap of a dog snuggling in against her side.

With no real sense of how long she has been asleep, she dreams of being doused by enormous drops of water. At the same instant, she realises that these drops are indeed falling from the sky itself and she sits up with a start, aware that the temperature has suddenly dropped. A colossal black whale-like cloud has formed overhead and is soon dumping itself down in stair-rods. She remembers her mother's warnings of how Exmoor weather can change in a flash and she scrambles to her feet.

Just at that moment Ruggles starts to whimper and tries to corral Sophie towards an open door and the figure of a minute little lady who is standing in front of a small cottage on the other side of the graveyard. "Now Ruggles, let that young lady come here on her own, you daft dog" she says. "Please do come in young miss and get yourself dried off. I'm Lizzie Cooke and you are most welcome to come inside until this pesky black cloud has gone over". Sophie gladly did as she was asked, and swiftly picking up her jacket and boots headed straight for the open door and the prospect of shelter. Once inside she was taken aback by the level of light which was very low as the windows were minute and the walls very thick. Lizzie Cooke however was bright like a spinning top with smooth dark hair and very rosy cheeks - she was simply but immaculately dressed and reminded Sophie of the lady who bobbed out from the cuckoo clock in her grandmother's house. With her pinny, bright cheeks and an upright stance, Lizzie was the essence of neatness, of order, and a certain cheeriness which seemed to promise good humour and care. In all truth she did not seem quite of this time or age, but neither was she a fake like that large woman who used to run a local tearoom dressed unconvincingly in bonnet and flouncy outfit speaking with a brash Midlands accent. Her mum had described this individual as 'very creepy'. Lizzie was undeniably real. Fussing over her, Lizzie steered Sophie towards the warmth of a hearty fire beside which she set her boots and jacket. But this fire wasn't quite right either because Lizzie was stoking it up not with logs but with what Sophie believed might be turfs made from peat, and surely that wasn't allowed in this day and age? Lizzie settles Sophie in a charming little wooden chair with patchwork cushions and in a flash draws up a little round table on which she places the largest scone Sophie has ever seen, and two small dishes containing in one strawberry jam, made from what she could see appeared to be virtually whole strawberries and the other of thick clotted cream. There was also a mug of something hot and fortifying, though exactly what it was she couldn't say. There was butter and a tiny little bone handled butter knife and a charming little china plate with faded roses on it. Sophie set to.

Whilst she was enjoying her restorative tea, Lizzie prattled on about how she had arrived in this cottage many years ago. Apparently, when she was scarcely more than a child she had ridden all alone up on an old bicycle from the depths of Cornwall. She didn't say quite why she had ventured on this epic journey but as she told the story, her face grew cloudy and she gave the impression that she had had to set out as a matter of utmost urgency. She finally arrived at this, her grandmother's house, after many hazards and ordeals and thereafter "I never did have the faintest wish to leave this place, nor I never will". Always an eager baker, Lizzie told Sophie that her scones and fairy cakes had become famous throughout the country and that she made it a point of honour to look after the folks who made the arduous journey up to Culbone church and to "set them on their way with a full stomach and a happy heart." Most were served on the little grassy lawn outside the cottage, but a few special people were invited into the cottage itself, the inner sanctum, and Sophie was one of these chosen ones. Lowering herself to speak in Sophie's ear, Lizzie confided that "I bin made church warden here see, and though I were told by they that owned this ground that I was to keep the church locked up, I never did see, and I just say the key bin lost. That's how I go on and will do, and no-one shall stop me!" As she clapped her hands together delightedly at the success of this childish subterfuge, Sophie joined her with applause. Ruggles who had fallen asleep in front of the fire, opened one eye disapprovingly at the disturbance and then promptly started snoring again. Sophie couldn't help thinking of the poetic justice of Lizzie contriving to reverse the fate of the poor lepers who had been kept out of the warmth and comfort in years gone by. In her heart she wanted to hug this bright, enterprising little person for setting right that wrong. In Lizzie Cooke's company it was impossible to feel anything other than settled and merry, and in spite of herself, she begins telling Lizzie something of her own story. She finds herself talking freely, and surprisingly, not at all harshly about her life and a little of her hopes and fears. It seemed perfectly natural to be talking like this although she couldn't recall ever having spoken of such personal things to a soul before.

After what seemed like an age of shared confidences, Sophie suddenly notices in the shadows beyond another very much older lady dressed from head to toe in black and with large black eyes to match. She was rocking backwards and forwards very slowly and seeing that Sophie had noticed her, suddenly gave an enormous wink and beckoned her with one gnarled and crooked finger to come closer. Unwilling to leave Lizzie's side, yet intrigued by this second figure in the cottage, Sophie rose and slowly approached. There was a tiny stool nearby and Sophie perched on that at the old lady's side thinking how wonderfully odd the day had been and wondering what on earth could possibly happen next to startle and amaze her.

Seen up close, the overwhelming impression of the old lady was 'leathery' and the dark wrinkled texture of her skin contrasted with her finery. She put out her hand and asked Sophie to lay her own small white hand in the grizzled upturned palm with its brightly flashing rings. Sophie baulked but then did as she was asked since there was something about the old dame that commanded attention and could not be refused. She had a feeling of surrendering to a force bigger than herself and as soon as her hand touched the old lady's skin there was a sense that there could be no holding back and that she was embarking on a deep journey of discovery. The old lady murmured many things to Sophie and asked her many questions which she felt bound to answer. But somehow she knew this was not to be the easy chatter she had had with Lizzie, this was different and would involve her in speaking of things she didn't even know she knew. In later years when she tried to recall the content of the exchange, Sophie could remember nothing specific about what had been said, but she did know that she came away feeling strangely altered. She was trying to work out whether this was a good feeling or not when she heard Lizzie Cook's voice from afar.

"You should go down and see Ada m'dear, right now she has much need of a visit from someone like you, see." Suddenly, Sophie was back again, very much in the present and aware that a long time had passed since she had stepped across the room towards the queenly presence in the rocking chair with such a feeling of trepidation. Now she felt more sure of herself and open to any eventuality. Indeed, she found that she was positively looking forward to the next phase of her adventure. So Sophie quickly gathered her things and put them on again, marvelling at how her socks and shoes were now perfectly dry. She hugged Lizzie who showed the girl out with the words, "Ada be very very clever see, but she lives too much in her head, that one didnums? Too much for her own good, worrying over those old sums and computations like. Be a fine thing for her to have a little visit from you, see? She be the daughter of Lord Byron and after Ada was born, he upped and went off to Italy with them other poet friends of his. Her mother though was consumed with rage and hatred for his ways and she swore never to let Ada see no poetry and instead learn only about facts and figures and likewise. She generally stays down by the sea, see, when it's fine. Sun's hot again now and that's where you'll likely find her. Ruggles will show you the way. Take this old stag's horn, when you want to go home, just twist the antlers round clockwise three times and follow on where he pulls you. Can't go wrong!"

  And so it was that Sophie set off once again, with the redoubtable Ruggles at her side, this time travelling fast downhill and taking the same path they had followed on the ascent. At a certain juncture in the wood Ruggles veered off to the right. After a while the pair found themselves passing through some mysterious tunnels, dank and oppressive and looking very like a place where goblins might live. They soon came out into the open, and skirted past a dark imposing house with many chimneys and three huge facades set back deeply into the wood. In spite of her unaccustomed feeling of light heartedness, Sophie was finding it hard to keep up with her scruffy companion. They passed through a yew hedge onto a little lawn and were met with the most bizarre sight. Ahead of her, in the middle of the grassy area, sat a large wooden cage-like object constructed in a series of hoops with muslin ties on the uppermost ring. Why, surely this must be one of those strange contraptions called a farthingale; she remembered seeing a picture of one of these in her History Book of Costume in year 12. But where was the owner of the extraordinary article and what was it doing out here on the grass?

    She looked behind her for the reassuring presence of Ruggles but he had vanished. Breathing in deeply and forcing herself onwards, Sophie took a large step through a second gap in the hedge and stood stock still. There ahead of her, sitting on the edge of a small rectangular bathing pool, which was filling up with seawater as the tide came in, was a young woman, not many more years older than herself, with her knees drawn up to her chest. She was wearing an old-fashioned skirted bathing suit, and lying on the ground near the little bathing hut was a fine blue tartan dress, clearly thrown off in haste, and beside it two tiny black patent leather shoes. Staring ahead into the water she looked for all the world like an alabaster sculpture. Her bowed head and air of contemplation gave an aspect of extreme stillness and resolve.

"Ada?" ventured Sophie, her words coming out louder than she had intended. She came around the pool and into full view "Ada, May I speak with you?" Ada jumped, and then noticing Sophie and her petrified look, slowly came to. "So you are here! I had a strong notion that someone like you would come by today, maybe you can be of service. You look strong and fearless." Sophie felt anything but strong and she was certainly not fearless. "You may know that I am Ada Lovelace, celebrated mathematician, and daughter of Lord Byron, the poet. My parents were not destined to live long together and as I grew up my resentful mother kept me away from all things emotional and artistic. Instead, she arranged for tutors to teach me only what pertained to the laws of mathematics for which it was discovered I had a great competency. So great by this time was her revulsion for my father that she would make me sit perfectly still for hours every day hoping with discipline to train away from me any unruly and dangerous movement that would remind her of my feckless father. This has been my curse. I do so long to plunge into this pool my dear husband made for my wretched health, but try as I may, as I approach, my body freezes and I cannot move. Is it so that you are able to swim?"

"Well yes I suppose I can," said Sophie, "It is one of the few physical things I can actually do with any confidence because I actually want to do it. I feel at home in the water and answerable to no-one. So much of life is about turning ourselves into the kind of person the grown-ups tell us we should be, but in swimming I have always felt I could entirely be myself. I've never really thought about teaching someone, but maybe the first thing, if you will let me, is to try and free up some of the stiffness in your body." She suddenly remembered the game she and Ruggles had played in the stream, in what seemed hours and hours ago when the little dog had playfully charmed away her anger through sheer mischief making. One more time, off came the leather jacket and the Doc Martens and socks and she rolled up her leggings and strode into the water which was slowly filling up on the incoming tide.

It felt amazing to be in that bathing pool which was just deep enough to swim in but shallow enough to be warmed by the late afternoon sun. Sophie reached her arms deep into the pool and lifting up her hands released a shower of droplets overhead as she raised her face towards the late rays of sunshine. She was in her element, luxuriating in the sensations of the water and saw that Ada had released her knees and was now sitting on the edge of the pool with her legs dangling down. "Yes! That's it!" Sophie cried out. "Well done, Ada. That's the first step!" and gently at first, Sophie began to direct little flicks of water towards Ada - Ada the revered, the august, the phenomenal Ada, who had been trained to suppress the impulses of her own body to shield her from the dangerous ravages of creativity associated with her mercurial father.

At first Ada was not at all sure about Sophie's 'freeing up' proposal and sits there stiff and guarded. Then she suddenly lets go of her fears and with an almighty shove of water chucked an entire cascade over Sophie's head and body. Sophie whoops with delight as Ada finds herself slipping into the water in spite of herself.

For one perilous moment Ada flails her arms in a whirring panic and looks as though she is going to lose her footing and Sophie reaches out her arms in support. Gratefully, Ada puts her own palms into Sophie's, and for a while they just teeter, slowly and steadily, waist deep, as Ada gets used to the unusual feelings of underwater weight transference and lack of gravity.

  Before long Ada wants to walk unaided and she lets go Sophie's hold and bravely strides out using little motions of her arms and settles into an easy rhythm. "Do you think you'd like to stretch out on the water Ada? Maybe we could get you floating. Don't worry, I'll support you. It's a delicious feeling." And with that Sophie lets herself tilt back as her feet come up to the surface and her body lengthens out. Ada looks on in awe. "I should like to do that more than anything in the world," she says, and without warning rashly throws herself backwards into the water. For a moment all is flailing limbs and chaos before she plunges down into the water which is becoming deeper by the minute. She finds her feet quickly and when she comes up spluttering and coughing she is also laughing. "I think perhaps I should have let you show me how you did that first!" says Ada. Sophie shows her how to put her head back and find that moment of tipping equilibrium as the legs lift up to find the counterbalance. Then Sophie comes behind Ada and holds her head in her palms. Feeling the contact and gaining courage, the older woman suddenly found the tipping point as her body opens out and finds its full length. It was a magic feeling to have Ada's trust, and Sophie moves backwards through the water from one side of the bathing pool to the other, changing the tempo, now fast, now very slowly, always supporting her charge. Ada breathes deeply and stares upwards into the cloudless sky where just the trace of a half-moon emerging could be glimpsed beyond the cedar of Lebanon tree. She is gazing upwards into the galaxy where her mind at once begins to name the constellations and start the business of astronomy but for once, this time Ada lets those thoughts dissolve upwards into the soft evening light as she allows herself to relax completely into Sophie's gentle guiding support.

At that moment of deep connection and mutual trust, a sudden loud intrusive and thoroughly modern sound shattered the peace. Both women jolted out of their reverie as the mobile phone in Sophie's leather jacket pocket started to ring insistently. Ada panicked and quickly righted herself by dropping her feet down to the bottom of the pool and clumsily making her way to the side. "Ada, I'm so sorry. That's probably my Dad wondering what's happened to me. They must be getting worried, I've been away for hours but I must get back home now. Let me see if he's left a message." She hastily climbed out of the pool and dashed over onto the bank where she pulled the offending phone from her pocket. With a start, Sophie realised the awkwardness of the situation, which had shown up more than anything else the glaring discordance in their histories. It was as though all that had happened that day had taken place, as it were, in a fold of time. But here now was her father's text message saying how worried they all were at home and that her mother was talking about sending out a search party since they were all convinced something must have happened to her. She must get back soon.

Meanwhile, Ada had clambered out beside her and seemed to be shaking quite violently. Sophie went to the open door of the bathing house and found a towel which she hastily placed round Ada's shoulders, rubbing her dry in an effort to bring back some warmth into this seemingly lifeless creature. But Ada was not so much in a state of shock as in the throes of a deep and all-consuming curiosity. She had gone ashen white and was staring at the phone, lying in its blue plastic Apple case. "What is that?" she asked Sophie gravely. Sophie explained very simply how words and images and speech could with this little machine be transferred between places miles apart. There was a long pause, then Ada began "My speculation was right. This is what I have dreamed of in my imagination and with the help and encouragement of my friend Mr Babbage, we are slowly beginning to find out how to take small steps towards seeing how such a thing might be brought into existence. Daily I work on the concepts and calculations. I have even had the notion that bars of music might be with clever calculations lodged and then transferred through such a machine!"

"Don't give up Ada," said Sophie, "everything you are working towards is significant. You are truly a pioneer. I will come again when I can Ada. We are going to be here for a few more days yet and we can carry on with the swimming lesson. You are already making great progress."

"That would be wonderful," says Ada "I feel I have many more things I'd like to share with you Sophie, not least of which is the fascination I have with my father, something that never leaves me. I already know that when I die I will ask to be buried next to him in the graveyard in Huxnall. My mother has tried to erase his influence from my very being, but I feel drawn towards danger and have already done some bad things of which I am not very proud. Come back soon Sophie, and we will talk again, and maybe I will soon be swimming like a fish, and feeling more at ease. I see Lizzie has given you the stag's horn, and that you are concerned about your family. Turn the stag's horn three times and you will be home in an instant. But please come again soon. With you I can speak from my heart and feel free of the conflicts which have so often made me ill and disconnected from myself. Maybe I can teach you some things about finding the middle path that will aid you in your young life." And with that, the women embraced, and Sophie turned the stag's horn three times and was soon outside the backdoor to her uncle's house near Porlock Weir, where her family were staying.

Sophie went straight into the kitchen where everyone were sitting round in silence, her mother looking pale and drawn. She had a phone in her hand as if on the point of calling to summon help. "It's okay, I'm back now and I'm fine. So sorry to have left you not knowing where I was and what was going on. That was really thoughtless of me. I've just been having one or two adventures, and I've met a few interesting new friends!'

"Are you really okay Sophie? You look well, different?"

"I'm good thank you mum, all good" and she went and kissed her mother on the head, something she had not done for many years. "I see you've found a stag's horn," said her Dad.

"Yes, it's a particularly lucky one, this. It takes you to places you couldn't normally go!" And she smiles at her brother who returns her grin.

Two hours had passed.

The light outside had faded, the cake was down to its final slice, and the members of the book club began to gather their things for driving home. Carolynn opened the farmhouse door. 'Good lord, do you have a shovel?'

One by one they came to the boot room to stare at the low wall of snow that stood sentry to their escape route.

'Not a problem,' announced Marthe, 'I've dealt with far worse. I'll push out and drive through, it's still fresh and soft, and you can all follow through behind me.'

And off she pushed.
Through the thigh high snow.
'Good ol' Mart!' they said.
They waited, listening for the sound of her engine. It started, they cheered, it stopped.

Marthe returned. 'No luck. Wheels are spinning.'

'Okay, okay, come back in. Anyone who needs to use the telephone should do it now in case the line goes down. Helen, do you need to call for someone to collect from

school?' *Telephone calls were made to family members explaining the delay.*

The host refilled the kettle and returned it to the range, taking a pack of crumpets from the freezer. People drifted back into the kitchen, some stood at the windows, looking worried. She wondered if her tenant farmer could he called to bring his digger to tunnel them out, the lane to the main road might also be blocked, but his priorities would be elsewhere, checking on the sheep. She opened her weather app: a light drizzle was forecast.

She put the hat full of names back on the table and drew out the next name.

4

Hurlstone Point

Graham's Tale

Elizabeth glanced out of the window, recognising that this was a full-blown Exmoor winter storm and could go on for days and took a deep breath:

"Most of you will have heard of the American in the village asking questions? Only yesterday he cornered me as I was waiting bar at the Top Ship at lunchtime, a busy shift so I only had a few words with him but he told an intriguing story. Well, it seems he had one of those hand me down tales which most families have of a grandfather who was billeted in Minehead whilst undergoing training exercises on North Hill during the war. I think you will all have seen the remains of the tank traps on North Hill and recognise that the area had an important training role in World War two? The American, I didn't catch his name, had one of those stories that might have some basis in truth but in telling from generation to generation had simply become a game of Chinese whispers with no way of separating fact from fiction. The only exception was a small black and white photo, taken in a bar in which six young men in US army fatigues are posing for a photo with a couple of young local girls, probably a dance on a Saturday night, a chance to relax and forget the relentless horrors, the rationing and possibly the absence of any local eligible young men. Anyway, the grainy, much folded photo, showed six Americans. Even without the distinctive fatigues they would instantly be recognised as from the US by the characteristic crew cuts. The American had indicated his grandfather in the centre of the picture with the sergeant's stripes. His central position in the group and relaxed manner indicated he was the leader of the group, stripes or no stripes on the uniform. The only other point of note was that he had his arm around a young girl, perhaps in her twenties, with a pretty face completely framed by unruly bushy hair.

The American had said he was leaving the next day and had had no success finding anyone who had known the sergeant or indeed the girl with the unruly hair. He did however leave me a card with his contact details asking that I contact him if I heard anything presuming, I guess, that a barmaid must hear much of the local gossip. Although I told him I had nothing for him it did bring back a story my grandmother told me about her work during the war. It seems she was called Cynthia and lived at home during the dark days of the early 1940s working as a coast guard volunteer. Options were limited locally, most eligible women volunteering to work on farms, as land girls as they were called. It was hard physical, but essential, work. Satisfying I guess, with almost certainly a sense of camaraderie as you so often get with a bunch of volunteers with a common purpose. My grandmother was unable to explain what had attracted her to the Coast Guard, but after some fairly rudimentary training she was assigned a regular position of Watch Officer at Hurlstone Point Coast Guard station. Cynthia, I was told, loved nature and the opportunity to contribute to the war effort and to do that on one of the finest perches on all of Exmoor was irresistible. Shifts were twelve hours long, midday to midnight when relief would arrive and the slightly tricky path down from the station would be navigated by moonlight, if lucky, and torch on the blacker nights. The routine was to arrive just before midday, hang her coat on an old antler screwed to the inside of the only door to the station and take up position on a chair overlooking the channel armed only with paper, pencil and binoculars.

My grandmother once told me a story of a particularly memorable day's duty at the coast guard station and since, judging by the view from the window here, we are going nowhere fast, I will try to recount it for you.

The war, although obviously not known at the time, was still in its early years in 1940 and the papers were full of the fall of France which had happened only a few weeks prior to this particular July day. Despite the news in the papers, the war had had limited effect on Exmoor. Yes, some terrible local losses of young men at Dunkirk, but food was not yet rationed or indeed in short supply. The weather was hinting at a long, glorious summer and life continued much as it had for all of Cynthia's twenty one years. Cynthia had set off from home, a small, terraced house at the foot of

Porlock Hill, a little earlier than normal that July day, definitely a Friday as there was a dance at the village hall on the Saturday and that had been all Cynthia would talk about. The walk to Hurlstone Point usually took around an hour but could take considerably longer, it was hard not to idle and exchange gossip. Cynthia always took sandwiches with her but alternated on Fridays with her colleague on the opposite shift to top up the biscuit barrel and called in at The Porlock Stores. The Stores were a focal point of the village and it was no different this Friday morning, the gossip was of the arrival of a small group of Americans. This in itself was unusual as it was still over a year before America gave up its neutrality and joined the allies so there was much speculation as to why they were in the area.

    Continuing her journey to work with an increased pace, it was unthinkable to be late for shift change, down Bossington Lane, over the small bridge over the stream and the long walk up the track, increasing in steepness to Hurlstone Point. Cynthia stopped as always a few paces short of the station and took in the shingle ridge below, keeping out the vast blue channel with the

Welsh coast clear in the distance. Dark smoke identified the steelworks which were fuelled by the vast coal fields of South Wales and, whilst Cardiff was not directly visible, the docks of the great Welsh city were the destination of many of the ships in the channel. Welsh coal was vital not only for fuelling the giant steelworks of the country, but electricity was generated almost exclusively from coal and not forgetting most homes had coal fires for heating. Of more interest to Cynthia were the birds; gannets, buzzards, gulls and if you were lucky a passing peregrine which nested on the cliffs. The flowers in July were still a delight, the swathes of Oxeye daisies covering the surrounding steep grassy slopes interspersed with patches of blue from the Sheep's-bit, the dotted spots of the unusual straw-coloured Carline thistle, the pink cushions of the Thrift and the swaying heads of great sweeps of Sea campion. With the background hum of the nectar gatherers enjoying a time of plenty, the war indeed seemed an abstract only revealed by the news on the radio. There was definitely no war here on Exmoor. Cynthia reflected all was well with life and with a dance the following night, yes life continued on Exmoor as it always had.

    Change of shift was a simple affair, the formality of signing into the duty log completed, Cynthia completed her routine of hanging her coat on the old worn antler coat hook, topped up the biscuit barrel with the purchase from the Porlock Stores and put the kettle onto the small burner for a brew. Binoculars secured and with mug in hand, Cynthia settled into the chair and placed binoculars, notebook and pencil on the adjacent small table. Sweeping the channel from end to end revealed no enemy ships and would be the routine for the next twelve hours. Just one watch officer for the twelve-hour shift caused some grumbling amongst Cynthia's colleagues but never from Cynthia. The metronomic sweeping of the channel through binoculars was essential work but to Cynthia it wasn't just work but a pleasure, spotting the occasional porpoise and the delight of distinguishing the rarer Common Dolphins from the infrequent Bottle-nosed Dolphins. On more than one occasion, with visibility reduced by the frequent sea mists, her heart would beat rapidly before the putative enemy U-boat morphed into the wake of a playful Grey Seal. The great coal transporters continued their passage, lying up until the tide was in favour and, with the turning of the tide, moving as one up to the vast jaws of Cardiff docks to refill and complete yet another cycle. A few small fishing boats came and went from Porlock Weir harbour, keeping the local shops and pubs well stocked with fresh fish.

The watch officer's log was not an onerous task, an hourly note of the weather and little else to record with just the odd spitfire returning from probably a reconnaissance mission up the Irish sea. Six in the afternoon marked the half-completed shift and the routine message of "nothing to report" to headquarters. With a touch of nostalgia Cynthia glanced at the levers for the old semaphore system linked to the arms on the roof now redundant in the corner. Cynthia had been trained in semaphore as were all coast guard recruits but the use of two ways radio was now routine since the start of the war. Perhaps some things did change on Exmoor considered Cynthia.

Another brew and a couple of biscuits and it was back to the channel scanning. The falling sun cast longer shadows and every scan seemed to be different from the last as the light shifted from its previous glare to a more nuanced softer glow. Bats emerged, just a few at a time but in increasing numbers as the light diminished and the air was filled with the twilight insect storm. This was the time for maximum alertness Cynthia had been instructed. Already rumours were whispered of enemy probing around the coasts and with France and the rest of Europe having fallen, an invasion of England was a realistic prospect. A few lights shone at Porlock Weir, and Porlock itself was lit up, but nothing unexpected broke the darkness in the channel. The rising full moon removed all colour, but the sea was still distinguishable from the great wooded cliffs of the Exmoor coast. Nothing stirred except for the odd rustle of small mammals and possibly the odd deer becoming more adventurous with the camouflage of night.

    Looking back, Cynthia reasoned that it first started with silence. The constant rustle of the small creatures of the night ceased although at the time the change did not register. The bats were no longer visible flitting in and out of the shafts of moonlight although, again, the mind failed to note this. The slightest hum in the still air was almost certainly the first warning that registered with a strange tickling of the hairs on the back of Cynthia's neck. Scanning the channel more rapidly, nothing had changed, no lights where previously darkness and Cynthia questioned her own senses, however the hum now had an accompanying vibration in the air and was all encompassing. The first flight passed over; Dornier Do 17, Cynthia's training cutting in automatically and recognising also that the new moon was perfect conditions for the enemy navigators to identify the most obvious target of Cardiff docks. Bombs were now falling, confirming the target as the docks, as the noise of wave after wave of enemy aircraft competed with the explosions rolling across the still dark waters of the channel from the docks which were now lighting up the night. Cynthia's training kicking in as she pulled on the headphones of the two-way radio and reported type and numbers of aircraft together with bearing. Night vision lost from the fires of the docks Cynthia could only return to her lookout chair with great care, not daring to use a torch, small steps feeling carefully for the cliff edge. The bombers must have continued north after dropping the payload swinging west and returning down the Irish Sea, presumably to bases in the recently fallen France. With mind working overtime Cynthia recognised that only through the use of captured French airfields would the enemy bombers have the range to reach Exmoor and the Welsh coast beyond. It seemed as though Exmoor was no longer distant from the war and the war had now come to Exmoor.

Very slowly the first rustles in the dark shadows around Cynthia indicated the small creatures of the night were venturing forth again and if it wasn't for the glow on the horizon from the burning docks then it might have all been a dream. Shift almost over, Cynthia completed the log, took her coat from the antler hook and paused to take one last long look at the still burning docks then, with determination, strode off down the cliff path as her replacement arrived.

The walk back to Porlock was normally a tranquil time to reflect on the minutiae of life and normally the monthly dance at the village hall would have fully occupied Cynthia's thoughts. Who would be there, what to wear and, having missed the last two months events due to shift requirements at Hurlstone Point, this month's dance would have been the only consideration on the walk home. Somewhat guiltily the dance did keep encroaching on Cynthia's thoughts, but she relentlessly pushed them away thinking about the devastation on the Welsh coast and the lives that must surely be lost.

    Reaching the village, doors were open and neighbours deep in conversation across fences, this was clearly no normal night as the village would by now have been as quiet as the graves around St Dubricius church. Recognising Cynthia and still in her coast guard's uniform, a small crowd soon formed around her. Exhausted from the long shift and the events of the night Cynthia's target was her home and bed but she recognised the need to relay to the growing crowd the events as she had seen them. Having repeated every detail of the night to the crowd twice and answered every question Cynthia was finally able to make her escape and collapse through her front door.

    The next morning Cynthia's routine would normally be an almost clockwork attention to details for the big night, check out the latest makeup colours at Porlock Pharmacy, new stockings at the haberdashery and endless gossip and speculation with her compatriots as to who were the band, who was going with whom and was the dress as daring in the hemline as possible. Cynthia had no regular partner and would go with a small tightknit group who had all been in school together and were still single.

Meeting up outside the village hall, Cynthia and three friends were soon deep in conversation and barely registered entering the hall where a small band were belting out Tommy Dorsey's "I'll never smile again" which seemed rather apt considering the events of the previous night. It was impossible to miss the group of American servicemen as they entered, a certain swagger defined them as much as the standard issue crew cuts. Cynthia's group huddled even closer, if that was possible, and there was no other topic than the Americans, a multitude of questions many asked at the same time but the big question was would the Americans notice them.

It was only the next day that the blur of the evening could be recounted. Not shy, the Americans had indeed descended on Cynthia's group and after an evening of dancing, drinking and tales from both sides of the ocean Cynthia had allowed herself to be walked home by the American with the sergeant's stripes. The subsequent weeks were a tail of long walks, tea rooms and further dances when shift patterns permitted."

The storm beat down relentlessly as Elizabeth looked up at the group and, taking a long glance at the fire, indicated the end of Cynthia's story as it had been passed down to her. The group exclaimed that that was only part of the story and there must be more. Elizabeth had never opened up about her family history before, but perhaps the empty bottle of Wicked Wolf was a factor or it was just the right time and place to unburden her family secrets. Settling back down in her chair, she completed the last chapter of her tale.

"It seems that the American had stayed several months before a posting back to the states. Shortly afterwards, Cynthia had secured a posting with a distant relative in the North of England returning to

Porlock near the end of the war with a small child of some four years in tow. The apparent lack of a father was not questioned in the later years of the war, it being assumed that he had been killed serving overseas, an all too common an occurrence. With the vague details of a marriage and grave in a remote Yorkshire village, no-one doubted Cynthia's tale as she returned to the routine of Porlock Village life now with a newly enrolled youngster in the village school.

That really is the complete history as I know it," said Elizabeth.

"Was the American my grandfather? I really do not know."

5

Mayday

Carolynn's Tale

Fernella-May breathed a sigh, a hot dusty sigh of relief that fanned her heavy fringe like a halo round her face, as the bus turned slowly into the Square. Passengers began to stand up and gather their belongings. The afternoon was lovely, the warm May sunshine full of its usual promise of a good summer, but most of them had been cooped up like her in this old boneshaker of a bus with no opening windows for nearly an hour, all the way from Minehead, and enough was enough. Even the fly that had buzzed ineffectually at the glass for most of the journey seemed to have given up the ghost.

She idly traced the fly's final pathway along the dusty rubber seal of the window with her finger, and, looking out, discovered a small drama taking place on the pavement outside. No one else seemed to have noticed, being too much occupied clutching their bags and trying to stand upright in the aisle while, accompanied by some final rattling and roaring from the engine, the driver manoeuvred the bus into place.

A girl, a tall pretty girl in a sky-blue dress, was standing at the bus stop, a canvas holdall at her feet. Her blonde hair was caught up in a high ponytail, and Fernella-May could see that she wore a pale gold St Christopher on a slim chain around her neck. She had clearly been waiting for the bus, because she held her purse carefully to her chest as if she was about to open it; but now all thought of the bus seemed to have left her as she stood quietly listening to the young man who had come to stand beside her.

The young man was equally tall – tall, dark and handsome, thought Fernella-May – and he was talking urgently and with great persistence to the girl who, Fernella-May could now see, was really a young woman in spite of her girlish ponytail. They are like Prince Charming and Cinderella, she thought. Like Beauty and her Prince who was once an enchanted Beast. Like every fairy tale there ever was. They seem made for each other.

The young man took the young woman's hand and pressed it to his cheek. His eyes glittered and Fernella-May was sure she could see tears there.

The young woman seemed equally upset. She had been looking away from him as he spoke, as if the words were too painful to acknowledge, but now she turned towards him and Fernella-May could see that she too was crying, small bright drops trickling down her cheek.

They love each other, thought Fernella-May. And yet ... something isn't working properly ... it's broken ...

After what seemed an age, the bus shuddered to a standstill and people began to disembark onto the pavement, pushing and eager to be on their way to whatever came next. Everything was fizzing with movement and colour and life again.

The young man had stopped talking. He reached up and unfastened the woman's hairclip, so that her hair tumbled down over her shoulders, veiling her sad face. He studied her for a moment, and then he seemed to move very quickly and decisively. He picked up the holdall, took her elbow, and led her gently but firmly away. Fernella-May hastily climbed down from the bus herself and watched them as they turned the corner beside the Post Office and disappeared from view.

She returned to her own present moment. She was expected to walk directly from the bus to the bookshop to wait for her lift home, and she always did, but at her own pace. She liked to look at things. She spotted a ginger cat sunning himself on the library windowsill, a cat she seldom saw, and she took time to give him some ear scratching and smooth head stroking. Then she said goodbye and walked on past the café with its delightful display board of Italian ice cream, past the gunshop, and then the antiques shop, to the bookshop.

Joan looked up and nodded briefly as the door pinged, then returned to her work. Rosie the dog was not in her usual place – perhaps she was off somewhere with Richard - so Fernella-May headed for the stairs and made her way to the window seat in the art section on the first floor.

This was her favourite place, ensconced with these big beautiful books in a quiet room that felt a world away from the busy street below. Why this should be, given that at fourteen she was still struggling to grasp even the rudiments of reading, was a mystery to many others but perfectly straightforward to herself. She had discovered a deep respect and affection for the books and what they represented – all that exploration and creativity, knowledge and wonder - that transcended whatever her own abilities were.

*

She had first found out about the awesome possibilities of books two years before, when she and her older sisters came with their mother to live in a small village a few miles outside Dulverton. The Sage family, who had owned the Dulverton bookshop for generations, occupied one of the big houses at the top of the village. It was impossible not to notice the disorganised but charming tribe of Sage children who roamed the village, nor their equally disorganised but charming parents, Richard and Louise. Fernella-May, by nature shy, and wary of small children who moved fast and unpredictably, tended to steer clear of them, but it was not long before Fernella-May's oldest sister Phoebe had spotted a teenage earning opportunity and made herself indispensable to them as a charming but extremely-organised babysitter.

One summer evening when Phoebe was booked to babysit, and their other sister Francesca was sleeping over with friends, their mother had to go out unexpectedly, and there was no choice but that Fernella-May should accompany Phoebe to the Sages. She was welcomed warmly by Richard and Louise, who told her that she should feel at home and make herself comfortable wherever she pleased. Phoebe gave her a fierce warning look to say: Do please be careful and don't touch anything! - but her attention was soon claimed by the excited children, and Fernella-May was left alone to wander.

It was an interesting house, with many rooms full of books and paintings and extraordinary things, and then there seemed to be even more to explore outside the house on that fine summer evening. Eventually Fernella-May found herself at a high stone wall in which there was a green door, enticingly closed but not locked. It led into a big airy outhouse lit by high windows, and filled with rows of wide wooden shelves. On the shelves were many neat parcels, all similarly-wrapped in newspaper and brown paper. Like a very tidy Christmas grotto, she thought, and struggled to contain her curiosity.

But the temptation was too great, and presently she lifted one of the parcels down and carefully peeled off the paper layers. Finally there was just a thin layer of white tissue, and beneath it there lay a gorgeous thing, a book unlike any she'd seen before, bound in richly-coloured cloth with gold letters, and inside the book there were wonderful pictures - coloured drawings of birds, and a great deal of ornate writing. It was quite magical, like a book of spells.

Perhaps I could just look at one more, she thought, and lifted down another parcel. Soon she was sitting on the floor in a sea of paper, with a heap of book-treasure resting in and around her lap. She was so absorbed that she did not notice the bright sky gradually fading and the shouts of Phoebe and the adults looking for her, until suddenly there they were standing in the doorway, watching her in stunned silence. Phoebe looked appalled. This could be very bad. Fernella-May smiled tentatively and said the first thing that came into her head: They just wanted to be in the light again, she said.

And somehow it was all right. Richard smiled back and knelt down beside her. He took one of the books carefully in his hands and explained that they were all meant to be in the light, to be used and loved, but they were old and some of them were quite rare. Their names were listed in special catalogues and he hoped that eventually people would buy them and they would be handled and enjoyed again, but meanwhile they had to be kept safe in this stone building where the temperature was the same all year round and the air was neither too damp nor too dry. The paper wrappings were like an extra skin, the same material as the books themselves. They kept the dust out and allowed the books to breathe gently – While they're sleeping, said Fernella-May, and Richard Sage nodded solemnly.

After that she was always a welcome guest at the house, whether Phoebe was there or not. She helped wrap the antiquarian books up again, very carefully, and understood that they should not be disturbed, but there were plenty of other treasures in the house to enjoy at her leisure. Sometimes Richard would show her a particularly important book that he'd brought home – I'll run it past the expert, he'd say, which should have annoyed her because she hated being teased, but she knew he was not being unkind, just happy to share his enthusiasm with her. And Louise was always ready to look over her shoulder and explain some of the difficult words, helping her to make sense of what she was looking at.

So it was only natural that last autumn, when Fernella-May started travelling home from her special school on the public bus by herself, and her mother started a part-time access course at the Tech, the Sages offered to help with lifts, bringing Fernella-May home from Dulverton in time for tea after the shop was closed.

Fernella-May found this arrangement most satisfactory. She liked the new sense of independence it gave her, and she loved the bookshop, with its quiet dreamy atmosphere and its maze of rooms lined with all sorts of books waiting to be lifted down and discovered. She liked Richard, who was often distracted with work, but always affable and kind. She liked Rosie the dog, a tall whiskery lurcher who was devoted to Richard and came to work with him every day – each morning he would throw his battered leather jacket down on the floor near the counter, and Rosie would settle on it for the duration, greeting customers she knew but otherwise snoozing quietly, dreaming of rabbits. Rosie seemed to like her too, and sometimes they would go for a walk together by the river after school. Somehow Fernella-May knew that Rosie indulged her in these little walks, which were nothing like her daily doggy tramps across the moor with Richard, but it was a companionable thing to do and added to Fernella-May's sense of belonging at the shop.

Joan was the third member of what Fernella-May had begun to think of as the bookshop family, although of course there were also other less familiar people who worked there sometimes. At first she had been a little in awe of Joan, a serious, sensible-looking older woman who manned the front desk most of the time and was always busy with paperwork. She had worked for Richard's father before him, and seemed to know everything about the business, and much more besides. Joan is Our Absolute Necessity, Richard would say. Just give her half an hour with the books and the telephone and she can find out anything. One day they will make machines that can tell us whatever we want to know at the touch of a button - but in the meantime we have Joan!

The first time she heard Richard say this, Fernella-May felt awkward on Joan's behalf, and studied her covertly to see if she minded being teased. But Joan just nodded with an unexpectedly twinkly little smile, and Fernella-May realised that she was politely acknowledging that it was true. She liked her for being so straightforward, and soon began to feel much more comfortable in her presence. She realised that as well as being a sort of superhuman lynchpin of the business, Joan was actually a very down-to-earth and thoughtful person who noticed everything, much as Fernella-May herself did. Under that formidable exterior she was like a rather fierce mother hen, making sure there was always a mug of hot coffee at Richard's elbow when he was lost in working out the accounts, and biscuits that everyone liked in the tin. On wintry afternoons when Fernella-May came in from the bus feeling frozen stiff, Joan would send her straight up to the office – The fire's on, she would say, and I bought some teacakes at lunchtime, so do toast them and you can thaw out at the same time!

The little office up on the top floor was Fernella-May's second-favourite place. In fact it was probably equal in her favour to the art room, but it wasn't always available to her if Richard or Joan was doing serious work in there and the door was firmly shut. It was just under the roof, with sloping ceilings and a small dormer window, and there was an old boarded-up fireplace at an angle to the room, where the green-tiled hearth was now occupied by a one-bar electric fire and a small Belling electric ring with a kettle on it. Beside the appliances stood several enamel canisters with tea and sugar and so forth, and a little collection of mugs, mostly chipped but always clean. The milk in its glass bottle was meant to live on the windowsill outside although sometimes someone would forget to return it there, so it curdled and they'd all have to have their drinks without it. As one might expect, there were many bookshelves crammed with old ledgers and reference books, and a tall metal filing cabinet and a short very ancient safe, but somehow there was also room for a large mahogany desk, where the large black telephone stood in splendour, dominating the squat fax machine beside it. Finally for comfort there were two old leather armchairs and a narrow daybed covered in an Indian bedspread and jaunty cushions. There was hardly room to move, but it was very cosy, which was certainly Fernella-May's main requirement, and she felt very much at home.

*

The drama at the bus stop kept Fernella-May puzzling away for the next few days. What on earth had been going on? But then her birthday came – it was May, of course - and after that, the half term holiday, and she had almost forgotten all about it when, perhaps a fortnight later, on another long hot afternoon, she saw the young woman again. She was walking - no, drifting – along the main street at a slow, thoughtful pace, about fifty yards ahead of Fernella-May, and when she reached the bookshop she hesitated, looked up, and then stepped inside. When Fernella-May entered moments later, she could just see the young woman heading up the stairs, and by the time she herself made it to the art room, there she was, sitting in the window seat, looking at a large book spread open on her lap.

Fernella-May didn't really mind that someone else was using the seat that she'd come to think of as hers. In fact after she'd given the matter some thought she concluded that the young woman possibly needed it more at that moment than she did. From a discreet distance across the room she observed that she wasn't really reading the book at all but was lost in some distant reverie, although occasionally she seemed to gather herself together and look carefully out of the window to the street down below. She looked pale and anxious and unhappy.

Alongside the intense curiosity she was feeling, Fernella-May noticed she was feeling an unusual pang of compassion towards this unknown but so-clearly-troubled young woman. What had made her so wretched?

She knew that she was not socially adept like her sisters, but Fernella-May was determined to offer kindness if she could. She composed her face into what she hoped was a reassuring smile, and took a step towards the window. At exactly that same moment the young woman, who had once again glanced outside, stood up so abruptly that the book fell heavily to the floor, snapping its spine as it landed. Without stopping to pick it up she moved rapidly towards the stairs, a look of panic on her face. She swerved awkwardly past Fernella-May and fled downstairs and out of the shop. By the time Fernella-May had recovered from all this sudden movement and was able to cross and look out of the window herself, she saw the young woman walking slowly back up the street, accompanied by the young man. Their arms were locked in a loose embrace. Fernella-May felt more puzzled than ever.

The next few weeks saw some moderation of the weather, and also in the pace of events. There was no more fiery summer heat, and no more drama, although for a long time Fernella-May braced herself to expect it at any moment. The bright midsummer days rolled gently by, punctuated by soft sweet showers that were over almost before they began.

Apparently the very next day the young woman had come in to apologise to Joan for her hasty departure the previous afternoon, and had paid for the damaged book. After that she began to appear in the shop quite often, sometimes browsing the shelves for several hours at a time, a habit that Richard did not discourage. It creates a more welcoming atmosphere, he said, adding - And browsers do buy, sometimes! So it was that Fernella-May often found her there after school and began to feel she was a familiar presence, especially in the first floor art room. They would nod to each other in friendly acknowledgement, and on a couple of occasions the young woman spoke to her, in a soft slightly foreign voice.

I'm sorry that I frightened you that first afternoon, she said. Sometimes I just get flustered.

And - It's so peaceful here, she said. I come here to think. I know I probably sound silly, but I do.

Each time, their eyes met briefly and Fernella-May smiled shyly, accepting the words. The young woman didn't appear to expect a reply, seeming simply glad that Fernella-May had heard her.

*

One afternoon in mid-July, just as Joan was ringing the five-minute bell before closing time, they heard a commotion on the floor below. Rosie would not stop barking, while a loud well-spoken male voice demanded, at first pleasantly but with increasing irritation, Is my wife here? My wife? Here?

The young woman's hands flew to her neck as if to steady herself; then she swiftly gathered up her things with trembling hands and ran down the stairs calling, I'm so sorry! I'm here! I'm so sorry! I'm coming!

Eve darling, you really must keep an eye on the time! I've been waiting more than fifteen minutes! Anyone would think you loved your precious books more than me! The young man was laughing as he said this, although Fernella-May thought he didn't seem particularly amused. Nevertheless he put his arm affectionately round Eve Darling's shoulders and led her out into the evening sunshine and away.

Fernella-May, peering out of the upstairs window to watch them go, felt something uneven under her foot, and discovered it was the St Christopher chain that must have fallen unnoticed from Eve Darling's neck amid her agitation and the general confusion. She took it down to Joan, who said she would keep it safely in case the young woman returned to claim it.

The following Monday Joan looked up as she entered the shop and said,

Your friend came in for her necklace. She was so pleased you'd found it, and she said to thank you very much.

Fernella-May scowled with embarrassment, but inside she was glowing with pleasure. Joan clearly considered that Eve Darling was her friend!

And, continued Joan, she left this for you as well, to say thank you. She handed Fernella-May quite a bulky package wrapped in brown paper, with some words printed carefully so that they were easy to read on a label tied on with string:

> "I saw you were looking at a book about the Exmoor red deer the other day, so I thought you might like this. I found it back in April – they're often very difficult to spot, but I was lucky, in the right place at the right time. My husband didn't want it in the house, and you don't have to keep it – just leave it in the

woods for the other animals to eat if you'd rather. But it is amazing isn't it!"

'This' was an antler, one of a pair that a stag would have shed earlier in the year before growing new ones for the autumn rut. Formed from bone, now quite dead but still full of valuable minerals and fats, it was smooth and white, with three elegantly branched points along its length. Fernella-May marvelled at its beauty, and decided that she would keep it for a while, at least until she saw Eve again and could thank her properly. She put it up in the office for safe keeping, on the mantelshelf above the fire. Everyone who saw it admired it and before long it seemed to have become a permanent fixture.

*

But seeing Eve Darling again soon was not a certain matter. The school term was almost at an end and seven weeks of summer holidays stretched ahead, with no need for her to be in Dulverton at all, let alone in the bookshop waiting for her lift home.

Fernella-May did her best to enjoy all the nice things her mother had planned for them, and in truth it wasn't that difficult; two weeks with her grandparents on the farm in Hartland, day trips to Taunton and Exeter, and a lot of fun and freedom at home with her sisters, who dressed her up, painted her nails and did her hair, and taught her the latest dance moves. They took picnics up on the moor, and messed about by the river at Landacre Bridge. They caught the bus to Minehead to spend sunny days on the beach, then played on the pennyslot machines and ate fish and chips on the way home. And there was a new litter of kittens at the Sage's.

By the time September came around, Fernella-May had almost forgotten the routine of school and was not too pleased to be returning, even though it meant that she could resume her pleasant afternoons at the bookshop and perhaps see Eve Darling again. However she soon discovered a special attraction of the new school year that she had not anticipated, and this was Sister Veronica.

Fernella-May and her classmates were beginning their last year at the school. The following summer they would leave to find their place in the world, whatever that might be. Sister Veronica's task was to prepare them for the adult life that lay ahead of them, through a combination of practical information and kindly advice, which she tempered with all manner of interesting anecdotes, historical references and personal experiences. The double lesson on Friday afternoons featured on the timetable as 'Life Skills in a Civil Society'. Fernella-May had no idea what this might mean, but she found it utterly enthralling, longing for each week to pass quickly until she could enjoy the next one.

The very first session had captured her imagination immediately. It was entitled, 'Help! I need somebody!' and Sister Veronica had explained that everyone needed help sometimes. There was no shame in asking for it, and there was plenty of it out there, from the Emergency Services to specialist organisations to ordinary members of the community, friends and neighbours. She made sure that all the students knew how and when to dial 999, and then she discussed with them whether you might need advice rather than help, though sometimes you might need both. She told them about the Citizens Advice Bureau, how to look out for useful posters and advertisements at places like the Library, and she encouraged them to notice the sort of person who might be someone you could talk to if you were having difficulties. Most people were very happy to help, she said.

Halfway through the lesson she broke off to give them what she called 'the interval talk – something interesting, just for fun!' She told them about the long tradition of helping travellers, especially those at sea. She explained how communications worked in the old days, about Morse code and SOS – Save Our Souls – and the international call sign Mayday, from the French 'M'aidez', meaning 'Help me'. They all laughed about the muddled language, though of course it was really a serious matter. And she told them some true stories of brave people who had responded to cries for help, including Grace Darling the Victorian lighthouse-keeper's daughter, who had rowed out to sea in a terrible storm to rescue the crew from a stricken ship about to sink.

Finally, to end the session, Sister Veronica turned to the subject of giving help. Of course you should always be prepared to give assistance to those less fortunate than yourself, and to volunteer in one of many ways in your community, whatever your skills might be. She suggested some examples – raising money for charity, learning First Aid, helping at a Youth Club. But it was also important as an individual always to look around you and spot when others needed help from you, whether it was simply carrying a heavy bag for someone who was struggling, or reaching out to a friend in distress.

Driving home with Richard that first Friday afternoon, Fernella-May was so fired with enthusiasm that she found herself doing all the talking, not something that happened very often. She spent the entire journey telling him about Sister Veronica's lesson, and would have carried on beyond, except that Richard had a meeting to go to. He responded in his usual constructive way - Right, I'll find you some books about all that. And of course he was as good as his word. On Monday there was a whole pile of books waiting for her on the window seat, and she spent the next few days poring over them, covering everything from a Morse code manual to a bound collection of the Illustrated London News which contained a report and some fine pictures of Grace Darling's heroism.

*

Meanwhile however there was no sign of Eve Darling. Joan volunteered the information that on her most recent visit to the shop, perhaps in mid-August, she had said something about going away for a few days, and she hadn't been seen since. Fernella-May was so distracted by her new enthusiasm that at first she did not miss her. But when a full week had gone by and still no sign of her quiet friend across the room, she began to wonder where she could be.

Then one rather wet afternoon, idly watching the rain from the window seat, she noticed a woman wearing a headscarf and dark glasses walking past on the other side of the road, and realised that she was Eve Darling. She banged on the window to attract her attention, but the woman did not look up, and did not come across the road to the shop. Instead she walked on until she was opposite the café, and then she crossed the road and disappeared inside.

Fernella-May was perplexed, unsure what to do. She felt a strong need to find out if Eve Darling was all right, and decided that since no one had ever told her expressly not to leave the bookshop once she'd arrived there, it was perhaps acceptable to leave just for a few minutes as long as she returned immediately. So she did.

Eve Darling was sitting by herself at a table in the furthest corner of the café. She was still wearing her dark glasses. Fernella-May opened the door cautiously. She had never entered a café by herself before. No one challenged her, so she crossed the room and sat down quickly at the same table.

You look sort of weird, she said.

Eve Darling smiled gently, but she still did not remove the dark glasses. I had a bit of an accident, she said. It was stupid really. Or rather, I was stupid. But it's fine now. Really, I'm fine.

They sat looking at each other for a while. Fernella-May did not usually feel comfortable with direct eye contact, and she did not feel exactly comfortable now, but it gradually dawned on her that she would not have minded looking directly at Eve Darling. It was the uncertainty of what might lie behind the dark glasses that bothered her.

Eve was speaking again. It's good to see you, Fernella-May. Thank you for popping in. I hope you liked the antler.

Then the waitress arrived with a pot of tea just as Fernella-May was saying, Oh yes, thank you it was amazing. So then she said, I'd better get back, and Eve Darling said, Take care, I'll see you soon. And Fernella-May said, Yes. You take care too - and hurried back to the bookshop and slipped inside before anyone even noticed she had gone out.

Two weeks later, at the beginning of October, Eve Darling returned to the bookshop. The days were getting shorter now, the sun was lower in the sky, and the lights burned in the shop from the middle of the afternoon. Fernella-May quite liked the cosiness that crept upon you during the autumn, knowing that you could draw the old velvet curtains across and hunker down in one of the comfy chairs scattered around the shop, pulling your legs up under you, and lose yourself in a good book. Without even discussing it, she saw that Eve Darling liked to do the same thing, and they passed several pleasant afternoons in this companionable way.

Fernella-May often studied Eve's face closely when she wasn't looking, anxious that the evidence of her accident might still be there, but she detected nothing. Her expression carried that same quiet sad look that she had always had, and perhaps there was something new now, a sort of wariness about her, but otherwise everything about Eve Darling seemed as serene as ever. Still, Fernella-May felt that something wasn't quite right. She wished she could consult her sisters about this situation that didn't really seem to be a Situation – they were so much more knowledgeable about life, they understood human behaviour and social niceties in a way she couldn't imagine ever being able to do. But instinctively she sensed that for now Eve Darling's unhappiness was a very private matter.

*

On the Thursday before half term Fernella-May was in her usual place in the art room. She guessed it was nearly closing time, but across the room Eve Darling in her usual place had not yet stirred, and so neither did she. Suddenly the peace of the shop was disturbed as it had been once before by Eve's husband looking for his wife. They could hear him talking loudly downstairs, and Joan's polite protests, and then he came bounding up the stairs two at a time and sprang across the room to Eve's side. He didn't seem to notice Fernella-May at all.

Come on Eve, what the hell do you think you're doing? We said five at the Town Hall.

He was almost shouting, but managed to control himself and started muttering at her instead.

Fernella-May felt sick. She disliked loud noises of any kind, and this man's wild aggression frightened her. She sank down further into her chair and closed her eyes tight shut. But then she heard Eve's quiet voice, gentle and cool, saying, No darling, we said five thirty. Please let's not fight. I'm coming now. And Fernella-May opened her eyes again and watched her gather up her things and move towards the stairs.

Later, Fernella-May found it very difficult to disentangle her every sense of what happened next, to be absolutely certain about it. It all happened so quickly. There was a blur of movement, a soft thud and a scream, and then a shout and more thuds and shouts and the clatter of the man's shoes as he raced down the stairs after Eve, who lay in a crumpled heap at the bottom, her coat and bag beside her.

Shocked beyond measure, Fernella-May crept to the top of the stairs and watched the scene below. She could hear Rosie whining persistently somewhere in the background. Everyone else in the shop – Richard, Joan, a couple of late customers – seemed to be holding their breath. She saw Eve open her eyes and cautiously stretch out an arm and then a leg. Her head seemed to be bleeding a little and she put her hand to it and gasped with pain. Her husband was kneeling beside her, murmuring incoherently, and now he put his arms around her and cradled her gently to him. Fernella-May realised that he was saying My darling, my darling - over and over again. After an age, although it must have been no more than a minute or two, Eve pushed him gently to one side so that she could move more freely. She sat herself up on the bottom stair and said to the world at large, I'm so sorry, I didn't mean to scare everybody! I think I'm fine, just a bit of bruising. And she ruefully rubbed her ankle.

Now Joan stepped forward with the first aid box. She knelt in front of Eve and looked up at her, so that Fernella-May could see her kindly enquiring face as she sought to establish what had happened and how badly hurt Eve might be. She seemed to lean forward at one point and ask something very quietly in her ear. But Eve looked at her and shook her head, and then kept repeating, No, no, honestly I'm fine, nothing broken and I think it's just a little cut on my forehead. I just tripped over my own feet, that's all. Very silly of me! So they helped her up, making her flex every limb to make sure nothing was broken, and sat her on a chair while Joan cleaned and dressed the cut on her head, and then her husband came forward again and put his arm round her saying, Come on old lady, let's get you home; and they went.

Driving home a little later, Richard spoke anxiously, more to himself than to anyone else. We really need to look at that staircase, make sure there aren't any trip hazards. That girl was very lucky really, and so were we. Didn't half make a noise coming down… There would have been hell to pay if she'd been badly hurt. They could have sued us…

Fernella-May sat quietly, letting the words wash over her. She wanted to tell Richard that he had no need to worry, that the staircase had nothing to do with it. But she felt numb, powerless. She realised that she was the only person who had seen Eve Darling's husband give her the spiteful little push that had sent her tumbling down the stairs. And who would believe her?

*

Fernella-May feared she might not sleep that night, she felt so churned up and restless, but in fact the stress had exhausted her and she fell immediately into a deep, dreamless sleep, waking later than normal the next morning with a dull headache. Her mother saw how pale and unwell she looked, and said she needn't go to school. Fernella-May was very tempted by the thought of a quiet day away from everyone and everything, but something at the back of her mind was nagging her, and suddenly she knew what it was. She had to see Sister Veronica. So she said, Don't worry Mum, I'll be fine, and managed to eat her breakfast and get ready, and even smiled back reassuringly as her mother waved her off on the bus.

The wait through the school day was almost unbearable. Her mind ranged out of control, replaying the ugly incident again and again, tormenting her with sadness for her friend and a terrible sense of her own helplessness, so that she heard nothing during morning lessons, and was unmoved by the usual teasing and silliness of her classmates at lunchtime, and even sat through the whole of Sister Veronica's session on voting and local democracy, including a most interesting talk about the Suffragettes, without absorbing any of it.

At the end of this final lesson of the day, as the students' high spirits exploded now that half term was actually here, and they rushed and pushed to gather up their things and go, Fernella-May stood quietly near the door waiting for Sister Veronica to gather up her own things and leave the classroom. She had no idea what to say.

But she needn't have worried. Sister Veronica approached her purposefully but without alarming her. She watched the last students leave the room. Now Fernella-May, she said, I was hoping you would stay for a moment. You've been very quiet today. Is something troubling you?

Fernella-May took a deep breath. Slowly, painstakingly, she tried to explain. She felt as if the words were coming from somewhere deep inside herself. She had never ever spoken so many words to a teacher before, not all at once, and certainly not about something so complicated.

It's my... my friend. I'm worried about my friend. I think they need help. They've been hurt. It's horrible. But they won't do anything. I think they're stuck. They say they're fine but I don't think they are... and I just don't know what to do...

Her voice trailed off into an anxious silence. While she was speaking, Sister Veronica stood very still, looking at her steadily, quietly, and now she nodded and looked down for a while. Fernella-May could see she was considering the matter very carefully.

Yes indeed, she said at last, being in a state of denial does make it more difficult - but

not impossible. She looked up, smiling.
Fernella-May had no idea what a state of
denial was, but she picked up the words
'not impossible' and stood waiting hopefully
for more.

Then Sister Veronica told her that simply by
being a caring and loyal friend she was
already doing much more than she might
think. Of course she couldn't actually fix
things for her friend; they would have to
seek help for themselves when they were
ready. It was possible they already knew in
their heart that they had a problem. They
just needed a little courage and support.
And so on.

Fernella-May's eyes were closed and her
face had gone pink with the effort of
concentrating on all these wise words,
which had tumbled over her in a rush. She
was not sure that she could remember
every single thing, but she felt cheered by
the thought of them. And it was very odd,
because she knew the nun had not touched
her, and in any case she hated being
touched when she was not expecting it, but
the whole experience of Sister Veronica's

observations had been like a big warm comforting hug.

So, Sister Veronica concluded, perhaps right now you can concentrate on helping them to find their voice, for when they're ready. Perhaps you can show them how to ask for help?

Fernella-May opened her eyes at this. Oh yes, she said. Yes I can.

And then - Oh help, the bus! Thank you Sister Veronica! And she flew down the stairs and out of the building and through the gates and down the hill, disliking the sensation of running very much but aware that somehow she felt a whole lot lighter than she had done just a few minutes before.

*

Fernella-May caught her bus and sailed through the remainder of the day, albeit in a rather distracted mode. She was thinking hard, and she believed that she might just have a plan. Of course there was no sign of Eve Darling at the bookshop, nor did she expect there to be, but she waited patiently for Richard and drove home with him in the normal way, and ate her tea and chatted amiably about plans for the half-term week with her mother, who was very relieved that whatever had been wrong with her youngest daughter that morning seemed to have cleared up.

Half-term itself was a rather dull affair. Outdoors was not very inviting; the best of the autumn colour had now faded, there was a lot of rain and mud everywhere, and the clocks went back so the days seemed even shorter. Phoebe had departed for university at Plymouth at the end of September, and Francesca was absorbed in preparing for her own university application with her bedroom door firmly shut, so Fernella-May was very much left to her own devices and spent a lot of time curled up on the sofa watching TV.

However her mother noticed that she did seem to have one project on the go, spending several mornings ensconced in her room, apparently practising her letters. On the first Saturday morning she had put her head round Francesca's door to ask if she would let her have the old set of revision cards she had made for her chemistry O level last year, if she didn't need them anymore. Her sister raised her eyebrows in amused disbelief. What on earth do you want them for? But she fished them out with good grace, and Fernella-May carried away the little pile of bright pink filing cards, all carefully covered on one side with notes about chemical equations and the periodic table and so on. Then she turned them over and took out her own collection of felt tip pens, choosing the thickest and most colourful ones, and settled down to work.

*

Fernella-May returned to school the following week with the fruits of her labours sitting quietly in the bottom of her schoolbag, safely held together with a rubber band. Each afternoon as she approached the bookshop after school she felt a little frisson of excitement hoping that Eve Darling might be there, or come in before closing time; but several days passed and there was no sign of her. Fernella-May began to wonder if her friend would perhaps never return after the horrible thing that had happened just a couple of weeks before. Nevertheless, each afternoon she set up her special display on the big table in the art room and kept careful watch at the window.

Towards the end of the week a chilly Exmoor fog descended, sitting like a dense blanket on both uplands and valleys and showing no sign of ever letting up. Dulverton's streets seemed even more deserted than they usually were in November, and by Friday afternoon Fernella-May felt quite despondent as she walked towards the shop. Even Sister Veronica's double lesson ('Finding a job', which presented some very interesting possibilities) had failed to rouse her. As she left the classroom at the end of the lesson Sister Veronica had caught her eye discreetly, cocking her head as if to ask if things were better; and although she had nodded positively in return, thinking of her plan, she knew she was now feeling a bit uncertain about it.

There were no customers in the shop and Joan was busy on her typewriter at the front desk. Fernella-May went straight upstairs and set out the books and cards again. Through the week she had perfected the scheme: the Illustrated London News book lay open at the article about Grace Darling, with a splendid engraving of her rowing through the waves towards the wreck; and beside it lay another of the books Richard had looked out for her, with a large coloured reproduction of the famous French painting The Raft of the Medusa showing the desperate survivors still waving for help and a ship on the horizon finally speeding towards it. She had arranged some of the pink cards like a border around these pictures, and there were more in the little card stand behind the display. Fernella-May was particularly pleased with this final touch. She had found the stand on a shelf in the office, left over from an advertising campaign for local traders and businesses a few years before. It was designed for small brochures, but she saw it was just right for her cards, and the most important thing about it was its label written in bold letters – Please Take One. The cards themselves all carried their essential message in large rainbow letters, drawn of course by herself.

Just as she was standing back to admire her handiwork, Joan called up the stairs to ask her if she'd kindly pop out again to post some urgent letters. Richard had gone to a sale in Exeter and had 'phoned to say he'd been delayed by the fog but would be back by six. Of course she would stay with Fernella-May until then to wait for him, but meanwhile she was on her own in the shop and the letters needed posting today. Fernella-May pulled her coat and hood back on and stepped out into the fog. The errand did not take long and she was soon heading back to the shop. Was that someone walking along parallel to her on the other side of the street? It was almost impossible to tell, just a shadowy figure and some echoing footsteps. Fernella-May shivered and looked away, glad to reach the shop door a few moments later.

 Your friend has come in, said Joan brightly. I think she's gone upstairs.

Fernella-May hurried up to the art room, where she found Eve standing with her back to her, looking down at the display on the big table. She was standing so stiffly and still that Fernella-May was all at once fearful about disturbing her, so she crept over to the window seat and watched her friend from a distance. Eve looked like a statue, except that after a while Fernella-May could see that she was trembling, her shoulders shaking, and tears were rolling down her stony face. This was not at all what was meant to happen! She couldn't tell whether Eve was very cross or very sad, but she certainly hadn't intended to make her cry. Time passed, a minute, maybe two or more, and still Eve stood there. Fernella-May began to rock back and forth on her seat in an agony of uncertainty and distress.

Then Eve turned and left the room. She descended the stairs firmly and decisively, as if she'd made up her mind about something and was now about to deal with it, perhaps walking out of the shop forever. This was terrible. The cards had been a huge mistake, - Fernella-May could see that now. How could she have been so stupid? She snatched up a handful of them and ran after Eve, calling out to her and skittering down the stairs. Oh, please don't go, I'm so sorry, I didn't mean to upset you! It was just a silly idea, I thought they might help. Stupid stupid cards!!

At that point she lost her balance, and groped blindly for the handrail. The cards flew out of her hand like birds, shooting up in the air and across the space between them, finally landing in disarray at Eve's feet on the floor below. Fernella-May looked at Eve and felt utterly lost. She could sense a terrible needy alien thing swirling and circling around them— was it Anger? And where did it want to go? Would it land on her, or on Eve herself? Or did it belong outside in the dark with the fog, and just wanted to be free?

*

Joan had been absorbed in her typing, but now she looked up. At a glance she took in the extraordinary tableau before her – Fernella-May collapsed in a wretched heap on the stairs, clearly very upset, and Eve Darling standing stock-still near the counter, apparently in shock, surrounded by a sea of little pink cards. Joan peered more closely. She could just discern closely-written small marks like symbols and diagrams on some of the cards, and very large letters on others - mostly, yes all, Os and Ss. That was it - SOS. They all said SOS in Fernella-May's round careful hand.

Joan took off her spectacles, rubbed her eyes, and then leaning forward towards Eve she asked in her best bookseller's style, Can I help you, my dear?

There was a long silent pause. Fernella-May thought how true that saying was, the one about being so quiet you could hear a pin drop. She held her breath, and then there was a noise like lots of pins dropping, and she saw that Rosie had stepped carefully across the bit of uncarpeted floor by the counter, claws clattering, and was now pushing her nose encouragingly into Eve's left hand.

Eve smiled, she couldn't help it, and then she looked quickly back at Fernella-May, who couldn't be sure but thought it might be quite a friendly, even affectionate, look. Then she turned to face Joan and whispered, Yes. Then more strongly, Yes, I think perhaps you can. Then very firmly, Yes.

Now Joan was magnificent. She drew herself up to her full height, spectacles dangling on their chain like a badge of office, and moved swiftly round the counter to the shop door. Producing a large key from her pocket she turned it firmly in the lock, reached up and down to slide the bolts, flipped the 'Open' sign to 'Closed' and pulled down the blind. Then she gestured gracefully towards the stairs where prescient Rosie was already leading the way and said, Shall we go up to the office?

Fernella-May had shifted discreetly out of the way as soon as Joan took charge, and now she watched the little procession heading upstairs. Somehow it had all worked out all right after all – mission accomplished. Eve had asked for help, and who better to assist her in finding it than kind clever Joan who could find out anything in half an hour? It was in the hands of the grown-ups now. Nonetheless she felt a little pang of regret – her role in the helping seemed to be over. She'd collect up all the cards and put them in the wastepaper bin. Perhaps I'll keep just one, she thought, to remind me, even if I'm not needed any more.

But she was not forgotten. Joan looked back over her shoulder, smiling, and spoke reassuringly to her. Fernella-May my dear, please will you switch off all the lights as you come up? I think we all need a cup of tea.

Fernella-May stayed quietly for a moment in the empty shop. Outside the fog pressed at the window, chilly, unwelcoming, perhaps dangerous, but in here she felt warm and safe. All around her the books stood on their shelves, steadfast and true, comforting in their timeless certainty. She smiled happily, flicked the switches to turn out the lights, and headed upstairs in the gently humming darkness to join the others.

6

The Swedish Girl

Maria's Tale

August Bank holiday weekend, a hot weekend and plenty of tourists about, ripe for the picking, so what do three 12-year-old lads do? Well, they take their ponies to Tarr Steps and offer rides to children and earn some money. Ten shillings for a ride halfway up the hill, 20 shillings all the way up the hill. Each lad leads each rider up and down the hill, all day long. The lads decide to camp down by the river after the first day. The money was good that first day so another two days and they will be rich. Only they need to eat and of course do the things they are not allowed to do, smoke and drink. This is before the age limit on buying cigarettes, so off they go, at least two packets of twenty per person is purchased, together with some cans of beer. They also decide to be sensible and purchase sausages and bread. Now ready for the campfire. It is really comforting to sit with your best friends around a campfire by the river and smoke and drink and eat.

Though the aftermath of this jolly little weekend was for some of them not so nice. Having smoked nine packets of twenty cigarettes over the weekend, one was not feeling so good anymore. Two weeks of sickness followed and a promise to never smoke again.

Tarr Steps is a place they know well, as all three of them live close by. Over the years they have all hunted the woods for deer and foxes as part of the local hunts. Picked up antlers when the stags have dropped them in the spring, running over the stones and, later on, driving their cars through the ford. The only problem with driving through the ford to impress the girls, was getting stuck and the girls having to lift their feet above the water slowly seeping into the car.

A few years went by, and the lads finished school, well, they left school, supposedly at 15, just before the age was raised to 16. One of them managed to leave at 14 as he spent all his spare time doing real work, like hedging and fencing and generally helping on the farm. Health and safety had not reached these parts of

Exmoor at the time, and the inevitable happened: a chainsaw accident. The lad dropped his chainsaw and it cut a large hole in his knee. So that was the end of his "academic" education. To him the outcome of not having to go to school anymore and do any exams, more than outweighed any pain from his accident. Now for the real life of work. Shepherding, hedging, fencing and of course shearing, and then for the nightlife with plenty of drinking and girls.

After three attempts at obtaining his driving license, he succeeded on the third attempt. Both failures were for driving too fast, something that followed him in all he did. No patience at all. At last, he was able to take the girls for a snog in the carpark at Tarr Steps, and then frighten them by driving at high speed through the ford or, as sometimes happens, getting stuck in the ford. As far as I know, none of the girls ever offered to push the vehicle out, they just sat there and waited for the drive to continue. All the girls promised themselves no more snogging at Tarr Steps.

The annual boatrace from Withypool to Dulverton took place in late

May every year. The three lads, always up for adventures of any kind, decided to take part. A boat had to be built: when they told me this story they always laughed at their stupidity. They built a boat out of iron and it was very heavy. How they ever thought it was going to float is a complete mystery to them as well, but off they went in their boat. The boat did not float, and there was very little water in the river, so they mostly carried the boat and ran it on the riverbed. The winners were a team of lads who competed at several river events, and they had made a boat out of plastic. A very light boat that they were able to carry between them without breaking out into a sweat. Still, my three lads were able to come second two years running out of 40 teams. Not long after the second attempt the river authorities banned the competition because it damaged the riverbed. So, what were the three lads now going to do: no snogging at Tarr Steps, no boat on the river.

    The next thing to try was riding, as they were all riders after a fashion, and all three had been put on ponies as soon as they could walk, and without saddles it was a matter of just hanging on, as falling off hurt. No such things as riding lessons for these lads, just get on your horse and ride. Ride was certainly something they could do, but not such boring things as showing, or show jumping. For them it was hunting and galloping as fast as possible over the moor. They told me a horse only has two gaits, standing still and full pelt gallop, nothing in between. I protested and said what about walk, trot and canter? The answer: Yeah, for sissies! The sport to have a go at was therefore rodeo riding. They all three entered with gusto and of course won trophy after trophy. This was so much fun especially watching the so-called riders who all knew about things like walk, trot and canter, how to jump and do dressage, but did they know how to stay on a bucking bronco, oh no they did not. Then we had the visitors who looked on and thought how hard can it be, especially the London fraternity, who were all very streetwise, and knew how to handle themselves amongst country bumkins. They only lasted a few yards out of the starting box. But the Londoners had some tall tales to tell in the wintertime around the dinner table. This bit of fun lasted a few years until someone thought it was cruel to the ponies, so that was then the end of that game.

Girls was now the only thing left for the lads to pursue and of course with marriage and family in mind. Afterall, they had done the fun bits, and were now working hard at their various farm work. Farming life is all about continuation of family.

The advert said: looking after two small children and helping out with calves and ponies in South Devon, please contact the previous au-pair for more information. That looks just right for me and not in London but South Devon, just perfect. So, I phoned up the previous au pair and had a long chat with her, she confirmed my initial reaction, this was the job for me. I got the address and duly wrote to the family and said I was very interested in the job. I did not really have any experience in either childcare or farming life, but I had a lot of enthusiasm.

My parents were lukewarm about the whole thing, but my friends were a lot more worried about it. They all gave me warnings of terrible stories of how illtreated an au pair could be. Little money and long hours and lots of hard work. Still, that did not deter me: ever since I was a little girl, I knew exactly my path in life. When I'd completed my A-levels I would apply to university to obtain a teaching degree, but first a gap year improving my English, after my teaching degree I was going to travel, then settle down and make a career of the teaching profession, and of course somewhere in this mix I was going to marry and have children, four children preferably, two boys and two girls. As you can see this is real Mills & Boons! Did things work out like that, well in parts it has worked out like that.

Back to the beginning of my saga and getting stuck in the Tarr Steps ford. I waited and I waited for a reply to my job application, but none came. I kept reading the adverts in the paper but nothing else suitable came up. Then one day a letter arrived from a lady in North Somerset. She and her husband lived on a farm on Exmoor and had one little girl who was one year old, and they needed some help with her. There would be the opportunity to ride and help out on the farm as well as looking after the little girl every morning. A reply was written the same day and I started packing and booking tickets. The ferry across from Gothenburg to London took 36hrs. We docked at Tilbury Docks and I was met by the girl who had previously worked for the family. She accompanied me to Paddington station and made sure I got on the right train to Taunton. In Taunton I was met by the lady I was going to work for during the next twelve months, and the little girl I was to take care of. I put my suitcase in the boot and proceeded to the right of the car. The lady looked surprised and said, Do you drive? Oh, what a fool, of course the steering wheel is on the other side in England as they drive on the left, though I had been used to left hand driving as Sweden had only recently switched sides from left to right.

So, my career in childcare started, and I met the lad. I think he said, as did a lot of others, I did not look like they envisaged a Swede to look: blond, tall and blue-eyed. I was short, dark haired, with grey eyes. Anyway, all swedes can't look alike. I got stuck in and really enjoyed looking after my little charge in the morning, after lunch riding and helping out on the farm. None of those warnings came true I was working for a lovely couple and paid well.

About two or three weeks later was my birthday and the lady with the child took me out for a drive over Exmoor. We first went to Lynton & Lynmouth along the coastal road, had lunch there and a walk about. Then we drove across Brendon Common, and we stopped and I took a lot of pictures thinking how very different the landscape was to anything I knew at home. Little did I know this was going to be my home in the near future.

The journey took us through Exford and on towards Dulverton, but halfway there we turned right and drove down to Tar Steps Ford. At this place we stopped for a cream tea a completely new experience for me. After tea we went for a walk along the river, and I was told about the bridge and how old it was. I was also told about the boatrace the lad had entered last spring and she and her husband had watched with their little girl cheering him on.

Not long after my birthday I was informed that the farm had been sold and they had bought a new farm in Mid Wales. The lad was going to look after the stock at the new farm until the farmer vacated the farm the following March. In the meantime, we were going to live with his parents in Swansea.

End of March we moved to Mid Wales. I loved Wales and the Welsh people they were so friendly and welcoming. Time elapsed and I and the lad became a couple, we moved in together and set a lot of tongues wagging, but we got away with it as, well what can you expect of a foreigner and especially a Swede, everyone knows about their ideas of sex and nudity.

The following November we got married as my visa ran out. We got married in Hawkridge church and had the reception in the village hall there. After the reception we left via Tarr Steps ford and got stuck as the water in November was very high. The lad of course thought he could drive through the water like he always did, but no, we got stuck. Water coming in, me lifting my feet and dress, he looking sheepish, but then his face lit up. Look at that, an antler stuck in the riverbank, oh I do so hope it might be the one I have looked for since I was a lad, to be able to get a pair to mount. He quickly jumped out and thought nothing of being wet and dug out the antler, which was buried deep into the bank. The lad examined the antler very intensely and after a long time decided this was the antler he had been looking for. He gave it to me and said it is a pair, so now we are a proper pair. It will be mounted as a sign of our marriage.

So now you ask did they live happily ever after and did my dreams come true? Yes, we live happily but that is because we have got through lots of ups and downs and managed to cope with the compromises. My dream of four children, two boys and two girls, now that dream came true but no career in the teaching profession. Instead, a successful career in accountancy. The lad's dream of being a farmer with his own farm, now that one came true.
The antler found it.

7

Mr Alexander

Pat's Tale

I was 18 when I first met Mr Alexander.

The '29 crash on Wall Street had done nothing to halt the growing popularity of the hunt, and there were always city visitors, prepared to pay good money for a day's sport on Exmoor. My father was increasingly impatient with the Londoners – and to him, they were all Londoners - no matter where they came from. Today the herd of Red Devons must be moved, so it was left to me to take the horses to the meet.

I groomed Kestrel, my favourite, to a background of lowing and stamping. My father crossed the yard, a cow prong in his hand. Kestrel fidgeted nervously, and I rubbed his neck, whispering to him to be easy. I had worked hard on Kestrel and his coat gleamed. I looked expectantly to my father.

'That gelding needs to be taught to stand, you're spoiling him.'

I moved protectively between Kestrel and my father.

'I hope he's a better rider than the usual Londoners,' he said. 'All they want to do is tell their smart friends in the city they hunted with the Devon and Somerset Staghounds. Doesn't matter that they can't ride one side of the horse. Remember that last one, Lizzie?'

I busied myself with Kestrel's bridle. I didn't want to agree, but, yes, I did remember the pale, drawn face of the young man as he sat stiffly on Bonny's back and hastily downed the port offered at last week's meet. After his fall, he told me he rode in Hyde Park and hadn't expected there would be hills. He hadn't expected hills! Exmoor was nothing but hills: deep bracken-filled combes and high heather-clad moors.

'Anyway, he isn't,' I muttered.

'Don't mumble, girl! Speak up.' And then, 'isn't what?'

'A Londoner. He isn't a Londoner. Betty, from the White Horse, she says he's Australian.'

'Oh Blimey!' He lifted the saddle and dropped it heavily on Kestrel's back. The horse and I both flinched. 'Better watch out, Lizzie. Make sure he doesn't run off with our best saddle, or the mare, or, by Christ, you yourself, girl.'

I looked at him. I didn't know what he meant.

'Australians! They're all convicts. Even you must know that,' he said, over his shoulder, as he left the yard, taking his stick to the russet backs of the bullocks pushing at the gate.

I saddled and bridled Bonny and found my gloves and whip. The kitchen door opened and I saw my mother step through. It seemed to me then that she was beginning to look old, that her back was becoming bent and her face etched in lines of pain. She pressed a piece of cake, wrapped in greaseproof paper, into my hands. She wished me a good day.

I mounted Kestrel, taking Bonny's rein over her head, and started along the farm track. It was a perfect day, sharp and dry. The beech of the hedges was turning copper and gold, and the heather in the distance was bright with hues of pink in the Autumn sun. Dropping down to the bridge over the river, I saw the village filling with people, some mounted and many more on foot. Kestrel began to jog and sidle.

Even amongst the crush of people, Mr Alexander was easy to spot, small and slim, framed in the doorway of the hotel, tapping his boot quietly with his whip. He was immaculately turned out in very correct and expensive-looking hunting attire. I approached and said, 'Good morning', and asked if he was Mr Alexander. He looked at me in surprise and I realised he probably expected a man. He greeted me with a formal, but pleasing, bow. He mounted Bonny with grace and agility.

We stood a moment, a little apart from the crowd, and surveyed the scene. The huntsman on his black mare was in the centre of the Green, his hounds barely invisible in the throng of people, just an occasional wagging stern. Many people I knew from the local farms, but there were others, I didn't recognise. Betty brought a tray of drinks and Mr Alexander accepted the customary glass of port.

'It's a good turn-out today,' she said, 'there must be a hundred or more on horseback.'

Alexander told me he had first come to hunt on Exmoor many years ago, soon after he arrived in England.

'Not such a big field in those days,' he said.

I pointed to the red coat of the huntsman, and told how the fame of Earnest Bawden had spread beyond Exmoor, bringing many visitors, from across the country, and indeed the world.

Alexander said he had followed the hunting reports in The Times newspaper. The replenished tray of drinks returned but he waved away the offer of a second glass.

Clearly he was not a visitor who needed the fire of alcohol to dare to follow the hunt.

I was about to ask how he came to be in England, but we heard the blast of the horn, and felt the buzz of anticipation run through the crowd, as Bawden led hounds out in front. The master nodded to me as he passed and I looked out for the two puppies, Crystal and Gaylass, I had walked the previous year.

We watched the ladies of the county in their elegant riding habits and veils, and the smart uniforms of the military men, then took our place in the remaining jostle of horses. Behind us were the farmers in their flat caps, man and horse enjoying a day off from the labours of the farm.

Kestrel fretted and fidgeted, trying to edge forward. A few motor cars nudged past us, as we turned up a track leading steeply out of the village. A bottle-nosed Austin Cowley, like my father's and the polished Rolls Royce Silver Ghost with Lord Darcy at the wheel, now an ancient bird-like man, too old to ride to hounds. I told Mr Alexander that the hunt staff disliked the new phenomena of motorised hunting, and had tried to ban people from bringing cars to the meet, claiming the smell put off the hounds, and the noise frightened the horses.

I went on, 'My mother says hunt people always bemoan progress. She thinks it's nice that people can still have the day out when they are no longer able to ride or follow on foot.' I stopped, wondered if I was talking too much, as my father often said I did.

Alexander said, 'Your mother sounds a rational and independent thinker.'

I thought about it. 'Yes', I said, 'she is. And I am often surprised by the things she says.'

'I would like to meet her,' he said.

Looking to how he sat on Bonny, he seemed to me untaught, but to ride with a natural ease. Where many of the regular hunting men adopted an exaggeratedly backward seat, or slumped in the style of the old farmers, he sat upright. I saw Bonny respond to his sympathetic hands. I realised he knew I was looking and felt embarrassed. Seeking to cover my confusion, I asked if he had ridden a long time.

'I can't remember not riding,' he said, 'my parents had a farm, in Australia, and we were put on a horse's back before we could walk.' That was how it was with me also.

The cavalcade of horses snaked up to the moor, and the pace increased as we hit the open ground. I glanced at my guest, then released my contact with Kestrel's mouth, and both horses broke into a canter. I felt the coiled power, as Kestrel fought me for more speed. He was young and excited, and I was struggling to hold him when a bird flew up from the undergrowth, almost in his face, and he plunged sideways. Bonny followed her stable-mate and now both horses were floundering in deep heather. I felt my balance go and saw the ground coming closer. I made a supreme effort to push myself back into the saddle and managed to regain my seat. I looked anxiously to my guest and saw that he had barely moved in the saddle. There was an ironic smile on his lips, but he did not comment.

'Sorry about that,' I said firmly, slipping my foot back into the stirrup, righting my hat, and taking a firmer hold of Kestrel.

The hunt located the quarry for the day. The stag was sleek and muscular from the richness of a summer's grazing, and fired up for the oncoming rut. He took flight and we flew over the open moors around Larkbarrow, enjoying the long runs for which the staghounds were famous and for which people travelled so far to hunt on Exmoor. The horses went well, Bonny appreciating a competent rider and Kestrel settling after the first few canters.

At the first check, near Warren farm, I found an old farming friend of my father's at my side, Morris Stanley, riding a big bay horse I had seen pulling the plough the day before. I said 'Good morning' to him and introduced Mr Alexander.

'Is that the youngster from Darcy's old stallion?' Mr Stanley said, nodding to Kestrel.

'Yes,' I answered, hoping hounds would move off soon.

'Going well, is he?' he asked.

'He's still very young. And quite nervous. He hasn't been out much, you know.'

'He looks quiet enough to me. Looks like a good one.'

Infuriatingly, Kestrel was standing perfectly still, ears pricked to hounds, looking every inch an experienced hunter.

'Perhaps I'll be having a word with your father,' Mr Stanley said as he turned away.

I patted Kestrel sadly.

We heard the yelp of a hound, and we were moving again. Kestrel settled into a gloriously long, loping canter and I felt as though he could run for ever. We crossed the lane at Prayway Head, and I spied the car followers. Some of the field split off, as the heavier and less fit horses tired. Riders with second horses would be looking to change mounts around here.

I felt Kestrel's mouth, seeking to slow a little as we galloped over moors I knew to be studded with bogs. Now a small group of us had become detached from the main field, but we were following the lead of an ex-Master who I was confident knew the ground. Startled sheep from the sparse moorland flocks of white-faced Cheviots jumped away from our galloping hooves.

Following a boundary bank, we reached the dark jewel of Pinkery Pond, its water contrasting with the pale grasses of the drained moor. We took the horses to drink and cool their legs. A buzzard wheeled in motionless flight high in the sky. We stood in a moment in the intense silence of the lake deep within the moor. Then the horses lifted their heads at the sound of the horn.

The stag had turned, and suddenly he was there in front of us, poised for a moment, catching his breath. He was majestic and proud, and I found myself hoping he would get away and hounds would not have their day.

Over Ilkerton Ridge, we then dropped perilously to the shepherd's cottage at Hoar Oak and followed the narrow valley, with steep ridged folds of hills and intersecting combes. Kestrel was starting to blow as we reached the top. I did not bother to point out the disappointing puddle that is Exe Head, the start of the great river's journey through moors and woods, farms and villages, and finally to the sea at Exmouth.

The hunt swung left-handed, and back over towards Badgworthy. We followed, but it was becoming harder to maintain the pace. Hounds checked down in the combe, and I heard someone say the stag had found refuge in the river. We caught our breadth and the horses stood, heads lowered, nostrils extended pink, and flanks heaving.

'Are we far from home?' Alexander asked. He pulled a gold watch on a chain from a pocket and flipped the lid.

I looked around. We had in fact run in a wide loop. I gestured over my shoulder. 'A few miles, four perhaps, in that direction.'

He patted Bonny's neck. 'Let's call it a day,' he said.

'Don't you want to be there at the end?' I said, surprised I suppose that he should not want his money's worth.

'The horses have done well and they are tired,' he said. I hesitated. For myself, and for Bonny and Kestrel, I was pleased. They were tired and, whilst I thrilled to the excitement of the chase, and loved to be one with a galloping horse, I didn't like to see the end. I knew it would be as quick as possible, and I knew the farmers wouldn't tolerate the presence of the deer if it wasn't for the hunt, but still I didn't like to see the beast exhausted and defeated, surrounded by self-satisfied hounds. 'And,' Alexander said, with a twinkle, 'I am not as young as I was.' I thought how difficult it was to judge his age. His face was not that of a young man, certainly.

We bade goodnight to the Master and to others around us and turned towards home. We let the horses stretch their tired muscles. Kestrel jogged for a while, still excited from the day, then gradually relaxed, and I gave him the rein.

As we rode over my father's land, I pointed out the farmhouse. Mr Alexander started to tell me of the eighteenth-century farmhouse he owned in Kent. It had twenty acres with gardens, farmland, stables and paddocks. He told me that he had owned several racehorses but had to sell them after the crash last year, and admitted that he still loved to place a bet.

I wasn't concentrating on Kestrel, and his reins were long and loose, when suddenly he put a foot down wrong in a rut and hopped lame. I hoped he would come right in a few strides, but he didn't. I jumped from his back. I picked up the foot, hoping for a stone I could remove. There was none. 'I don't know what to do,' I said, torn between my responsibility to my guest and to my horse. I thought of my father, and what he might say, and felt whatever choice I made would be wrong.

Alexander took charge. 'We will take the horses straight home.' He offered to walk while I rode the mare.

'No, no,' I said quickly, before he could dismount, imagining what my father would say to that. 'You must ride. I will walk.'

I led Kestrel back to the farmhouse. Mother came running into the yard, an anxious look on her face. She looked rather sharply at my companion, then offered tea in the kitchen while I settled the horses in their stables. Taking off my jacket, and letting my hair fall loose from the hairnet, I found the squashed cake in my pocket and divided it between the horses, with a mouthful for myself.

The remains of the rest of the cake were on a plate on the table, with empty teacups, when I returned. Mother topped up the teapot for me and I sat down, collapsing back in my favourite kitchen chair. The old clock on the dresser told me we had been riding for four hours but I noticed how Alexander sat in the same easy yet upright way as he rode. Apart from a few spots of mud on his breeches, he seemed to be as fresh as when I first spotted him outside the White Horse. Away from the horses, however, I sensed he was not a man for small talk. His answers to my mother's queries about the day's sport were polite but brief. Then she asked what had brought him to England from his native Australia.

He told us of his passion for acting and how he loved to recite, but of recurring problems with his voice. When the doctor could not help, but agreed that it was probably something he was himself doing whilst reciting, Alexander decided to investigate for himself. I had the impression this was a long task of much patience and perseverance, and I felt my admiration grow for this fascinating man. I could not imagine anyone I knew approaching a problem in the way he described. I could not imagine myself believing in my ability to solve a problem. His discoveries led him to see that others shared his problem, not in acting necessarily, but in all activities. He found he could teach people to 'do away with physical and nervous strain' – I glanced at my mother at this point – and bring about an 'improved condition of psycho-physical functioning.'

His story was compelling, but I found it more difficult to understand as, I think, did

Mother, when he started to speak more abstractly, referring to the 'means-whereby' and 'employing conscious reasoning processes'.

Mother said, 'I fear that now, Mr Alexander, you are being too clever for country people like us.'

A moment of frustration crossed his face, quickly followed by the return of that elfish smile.
'Then let me demonstrate my method to you.'

He took one of our kitchen chairs and placed it in the centre of the room. He patted the seat and nodded to me. I glanced nervously to the door.

Mother said, 'Your father will be some time yet. One of the bullocks has taken a fence down in Long Field.'

I moved to the chair and he stood behind me. His fingers were slim and long, and his touch light and cool on my neck and throat. The aches of the day melted. He made the slightest movement to my head, with the same light authority with which he held Bonny's reins, and I felt my neck to be longer. An old ache I didn't know I had, a memory of a distant fall, dissolved and disappeared. My shoulders eased apart. His moved his hands to my sides and said, 'you do like to pull yourself down, don't you?' I didn't know if I was supposed to answer. I wasn't aware that I 'pulled myself down', I didn't even know if I was sure what it meant. But then I felt my torso lengthen and a sensation of space between the bottom of my ribs and to the top of my pelvis, as if there was an extra segment of my body where none had existed before.

'It's strange'. I began then stopped. I felt my whole body re-arrange itself. I had sensations of time expanding and possibilities opening up. I frowned, then laughed.

'There you go,' he murmured, and before I knew it I was out of the chair and standing. I was silk spun from his fingers.

'I don't usually allow a single lesson. It is unlikely that anyone can learn the work in one session. I can give no more than an insight into what is possible. I don't want to hear that someone had one lesson only and then went around telling people my method does not work.'

'We won't do that,' my mother said. 'I can see the difference in Lizzie. It's lovely. She seems, I don't know, somehow more the person she really is.' He nodded happily. 'To learn properly, you need to come to me in London. You need to come every day for a few weeks.'

I couldn't imagine such a thing was possible. But my mother murmured, 'maybe, maybe we will someday.'

And then it was her turn. I watched and I could not believe what I saw. I saw the years stripped away, and I saw my mother as a young woman, as in the wedding photograph on the mantel: tall, erect and beautiful. It brought tears to my eyes. A look of puzzlement crossed her face.

'It doesn't hurt anymore' she said, feeling her back, as if looking for where the pain had gone, and repeated, 'it doesn't hurt anymore.' She looked up to him with dog-like eyes of gratitude.

He said, 'No, and there is no reason it should ever again'.

'It's amazing, absolutely amazing,' was all I could articulate.

We did not hear my father approach, and we must have made a strange sight for him, as he flung the door open and caught my words. My mother quickly rose and made to appear busy at the range. I shrank into my chair. Only Alexander remained unreactive, the elfish twinkle in his eyes undimmed, and the same slight smile still playing on his lips. Very much in his own time, he stood to greet my father.

Father nodded to Alexander and then to me, 'I hope she's not been bothering you with her chatter. To me he said, 'it's the sport he's paying for, not to listen to a silly girl like you.'

And I crawled into myself, full of doubt. Had I talked too much? Had it not been our guest's idea to demonstrate his method to us?

Father felt the teapot, long gone cold, and Mother offered another brew. He refused. She opened the lower oven door and released the promising smell of my father's favourite venison stew. 'Did you manage to mend the fence?' she ventured.

'Damned beasts. Took down the whole section. I'll have to go back. They'll be ruining that next field.'

Alexander stood, preparing to leave. I was relieved, I wanted him to go. I felt ashamed.

Mother counted potatoes from the rack. 'You're welcome to stay to eat,' she said, but there was no warmth in her invitation.

'No, thank you, Ma'am,' he said, 'my table is booked at the hotel.'

'Shall I take him down the road, Jim?' she offered to my father.

My father growled in his throat, in a way that reminded me of the old bull, and pulled his coat from the peg. The door closed behind them and we heard the car starting up. I looked to my mother and felt myself breathe again.

Tired as I was that night, I lay awake, worrying about the future and wondering over the past. I listened to the sounds of the night: my mother padding about in the kitchen below, and the calls of owls across the trees. I worried about Kestrel: would he be sound? would I be able to keep him? I worried about my mother: the way she worked so hard and received so little thanks. I wondered why she put up with it all.

I heard a distant scream as a fox found prey. My thoughts drifted and I remembered how things had not always been this way. I remembered how my father would lift me up on the broad back of his horse, and I would accompany him around the flocks. Then the little Exmoor pony he bought on my birthday. And how he told everyone I was his best little rider: no combe too steep, no day too cold, how I never cried when I fell off. And then how he praised me for my cleverness at school, asking me read to him in the winter evenings, sitting on his knee in the big old armchair. It was as his constant companion that I learned the ways of the farm, feeding the motherless lambs, and placing my small hands inside a struggling ewe, feeling for the tiny legs, and pulling the new life free. I was his girl and pleasing him was easy.

8

Walking Exmoor
(Or do I mean rambling about on Exmoor)

Angie's Tale

When the Covid pandemic struck and we were all limited in the time we were allowed to spend outdoors, it made me reflect on years of walking on Exmoor without restraint. How did this lifestyle come about? There was the new job, a need to find somewhere to live, setting a maximum of 20 miles for my journey each way to work and finding a house which was 19.6 miles from my workplace, so it just fitted my criterion. This meant 35 minutes driving unless I was held up by a flock or herd of whatever was roaming along the lanes.

One of our first walks on Exmoor in the vicinity of our future home was whilst we were living in a rental property in Bratton Fleming and this could have cast a shadow over the start of our lives on Exmoor, for little did we know that 100 yards from our route was a body of a woman who had been murdered by her husband and left hidden amongst sedges on the wet peatland. Another walk around that time demonstrated the unusual and dangerous nature of the rare ecosystems of heather moorland and peat bogs, when one leg sank up to my groin as I walked along. Fortunately, I had two arms and one leg, as well as my husband, if needed, to haul myself out.

When we moved into our remote Exmoor cottage, there was much talk about the Exmoor beast; a large cat resembling a puma. We never saw it, but several sane people reckoned that they had. It is often said that there is a real feeling of remoteness when walking on Exmoor and the possibility of a large cat lurking created an added sense of unease.

An early favourite walk was to go straight from the house and over the open moor and then dip down into Badgworthy Water; the home of the fictional Doones. But, were they real? The remains of houses in this remote valley are attributed to the hermits of Bagwordia, but history and fiction appear to be intertwined in the stories that are written down.

Not many houses are like ours, in being actually on the open moorland ie. being sited between the cattle grids that prevent grazing animal walking off the moor. This has led to some interesting happenings. I arrived home one day from work to find a sheep in the kitchen, quite restlessly walking around the island unit, having come through the glass of the kitchen window which is at ground level, apparently skidding over the sink unit and arriving on the floor. My neighbour with the wisdom of Exmoor farming stock said that it was an accident waiting to happen because my windowpanes were too clean, presumably encouraging sheep to look in at their reflections and then slip!

On another occasion, we arrived home from a short holiday to find six sheep and four large Devon Red cows, all within the garden which we had lovingly created from a field. Sheep are good at going out the way that they have come in, so it was simply a case of opening all the gates to the lane and field, to enable them to return to the moor.

The cows, however, stumbled around our steeply-sloped garden undermining banks which led to some rethinking of paths and borders to bring the garden back up to National Garden Scheme opening standard.

We came to Exmoor with just a cat, but with four acres of land we expanded our "pets" to include chickens and a llama called Vicar. I hoped to be able to go walking on Exmoor with Vicar, complete with panniers for picnics, but our llama had been an important stud male and had lived alone except when needed for essential stud duties on the MacAlpine estate and so had not been trained to take part in such chummy past-times. Nor could we handle the female llama that we later bought to provide company for him, so walks were out, however they both enjoyed coming up from the field into the garden and sitting on the lawn in front of the house, which made a strange sight. On one occasion Vicar tried his teeth at gardening, neatly lifting a plant that I had just planted. However, their most entertaining habit was when they mated, always in front of the house and on a Sunday morning when they would make a bizarre "orgling" sound.

I suppose it was inevitable that we should end up sharing our lives with Border Collies; such beautiful and intelligent animals, bred to work with man and sheep and so, unlike llamas, keen to understand and interpret the needs of their owners. Not only did our dogs walk everywhere with me, but it was rare to even step outside of the house without a dog or dogs by my side. If it as a day for gardening, Muffin, our dear dog for sixteen years, would stay close by throughout the day despite having acres of space to run in, but as soon as it was time for putting away tools, he would run to the gate and look back at me as much as to say "It's my time now" and off we would go for a walk even though my Fitbit reading was already high. Car-trained, house and hotel trained and with a passport, Muffin travelled much more widely that Exmoor. We walked in France where hunters are allowed to stalk and shoot game and I was advised to "wear something orange" by the locals so that I wouldn't get shot, which didn't give me much confidence. We also did long distance walks together; the 25 mile Five Valleys walk in Gloucestershire, near my birthplace, and here on Exmoor, the Perambulation, a walk of 33 miles, which he completed with me on four occasions.

The Perambulation started in 1298 and involves walking the boundary of the Royal Forest of Exmoor, which was an area protected for hunting. Strict rules applied to the use of this area and various physical structures were used as boundary markers; walls, ancient barrows and stones as well as trees. It is a tough walk, mostly remote and difficult to navigate. Muffin would walk beside me, but at one point he began sinking into a peat bog though barely six feet from where I was walking, such is the challenging nature of the terrain. Even sheep get into trouble sometimes. Early on in the Perambulation on one occasion, there was a sheep in mid-river of Badgeworthy Water, so of course, it was a case of boots off and wading in to haul her out.....not great when you are walking for eleven hours to use up energy in this way, but looking out for sheep is something we get used to doing on Exmoor particularly in spring time when anxious lambs and ewes need to be re-united when they have become separated by broken fences and thin hedges. Walkers and dogs who complete the Perambulation receive a certificate and these are well-earned.

Twelve years after moving to Exmoor, I started to take part in another walking challenge; the ancient Camino, from St Jean Pied de Port in France over the Pyrenees and across the north of Spain to Santiago de Compostela, walking in the steps of pilgrims. Those that can devote the necessary 4-6 weeks to walk the Camino in one go can immerse themselves totally in this unique experience, however our stints of eight days walking carrying backpacks of essential belongings honed down to 6 kilograms still provided a very special experience of journeying across the countryside with nothing else to think about other than following the route (indicated by yellow arrows or shells), making sure you were able to continue by caring for feet, applying sunscreen and drinking water. Beyond these simple matters, there was the camaraderie amongst the pilgrims or " peregrinos" as we were called, along the way and in the refugios where we slept and for some it was a profound religious experience and if not that, at least something quite spiritual. It is difficult to capture the same depth of feeling when walking on Exmoor, as the day-to-day chores that await the return from a walk can intrude on one's mind. However, the unspoilt, quiet and timeless nature of the landscape can quickly transport one's thoughts away from the mundane.

We have a much-used book that describes the archaeology of Exmoor and defines in an appendix where features can be found, giving 8-figure grid references. Many times I have walked across moorland, compass in hand pacing out distances to find a small stone and then another, often partly hidden in sedge, heather or gorse and realising that they form a stone circle or other type of stone setting, not magnificent like Stonehenge, but special in that there is nothing to say that they are there, no interpretation board or sign and I feel as if I am the first person to have discovered this ancient place. Why are they there? "Ritual" is a common explanation in archaeology, although it gives little explanation. The important thing is that one feels an amazing link with the past and the people who have also walked here years ago. I don't need to walk far to get that link with the past, for as I sit in bed I look out towards the corner of a field where one of only three Bronze Age Exmoor hand axes was found, so maybe when I walk around the garden I am walking in the footsteps of Bronze Age man.

Bronze Age man has left behind some larger features on Exmoor, namely the massive ridgeway barrows which stand out on the horizons. These inevitably attracted attention and there have been those in the past who have walked out to them to dig into them to reveal their secrets and the dips in their conical shapes bear witness o this intrusion. As a teenager, I accompanied my parents and other keen folk on Sunday afternoons to visit archaeological sites, that they had learnt about in their evening lecture during the preceding week. A few years ago, I had the chance to assist a PhD student on an archaeological dig on Brendon Common, here on Exmoor. Lidar had suggested that the site might reveal something interesting, but when the turf had been cleared off, it was difficult to interpret what one might be looking at. One helper took part in digs in Israel each year and seemed used to regularly revealing significant finds, maybe a goblet or something of that ilk, but we soon realised that, on Exmoor, we needed to focus on much smaller things, like charcoal. However, when I excitedly found a piece of charcoal less than 1mm in size, it was apparently the wrong sort of charcoal! Nevertheless, my interest in archaeology has remained, stimulating walks to barrows and stone settings and cists.

Others on Exmoor are searching out very different things when they go walking, like my friend who can identify 170 species of dandelion and therefore has his attention fixed firmly on the ground. Another friend seeks out unusual and old varieties of apple trees on Exmoor farmland and by taking cuttings, called scions and grafting them onto rootstocks for friends to grow on, he is ensuring that these interesting remnants of the past live on.

When the Covid pandemic struck, walking in remote parts of Exmoor where others tend not to go, seemed a wise idea. At a time when our own community had effectively ceased to function, it was interesting that we sought out abandoned medieval settlements to walk to, that may now exist only in the form of a few walls partly obscured by vegetation or even just a section of rectangular bank, easily missed, which defines where someone's home was sited. One can only imagine what life was like in these lonely and beautiful places. Was life always idyllic? There are chilling tales of murder and mystery on Exmoor. A walk along the River Barle east from Simonsbath leads one to the site of the Wheal Eliza mine along with the remains of the miners' cottages still visible. Here a search was organised to find a missing girl.

She was part of a family of four; Mum, Dad and two children living in a concealed valley which drops down to the River Barle. There are no roads here, just a walkway down past a small quarry where the father worked, which is still clearly visible. With a compass and counting paces, the site of their home can be imagined but to be honest, there are no clear remains. The mother died, the elder child went into service and the younger child was then in the sole care of her father, who moved into a shared lodging on the Simonsbath to

Exford road. What happened is not certain, but when the child was no longer there, her father told people that she was being cared for by people in Porlock. One local man was not convinced and was determined to find out what had happened to her. He succeeded in raising enough money to have the Wheal Eliza mine drained of water and this tragically revealed the body of the missing child. Her father, William Burgess, was tried and hanged whilst Anna is lain to rest in the churchyard at Simonsbath.

A church not to be missed is Culbone, the smallest church in England, isolated and magically set within woods on the cliffs between Lynton and Porlock. It can be reached by walking along the Southwest coast path. There is a real sense of the past here. In 1544, 45 lepers were banished to the woods here and made charcoal which they traded across the stream that runs through the churchyard; the barrier between them and the rest of the world. Two centuries earlier, French prisoners of war were confined in the woods around Culbone.

World War II has left its mark on Exmoor, as a training ground and an experimental area; a place of tanks, rocket launches and stores of mustard, chlorine and phosgene gases. There was a base just a few hundred yards from our home at Cross Gate on Brendon Common. Nine buildings housed soldiers from America, Canada and New Zealand. I often walk around the lumps and bumps in the ground which are the remains of these buildings and other structures with bits of concrete and brick walls as well as sundry metal objects still evident in the grass.

The soldiers augmented their limited food supplies by buying rabbits from local rabbit catchers who paid farmers rent to set traps on their land. The so called "rabbit acreage " was very valuable. Beyond the remains of the base, one can walk along the deep trenches where the tanks went out over the moor to practice shelling. Old Exmoor homesteads like Larkbarrow and Tom's Hill were destroyed as a result. Fortunately, some sites were identified as worthy of protection by the erection of an iron cross and these are still visible today.

A walk southwards from the base leads to the experimental area on Brendon Common where the Royal Engineers trialled rockets. One can follow old concrete post alignments stretching out across the moor, which defined the zone for rocket firing. Sadly, Col. Maclaren who was commander of the base was killed here, having thrown himself onto the rocket launcher to protect his men. A memorial stands high on the skyline to mark his memory. This was a base shrouded in secrecy. Some believe an experiment was done here of "rain making" which could have led to cloud formation and subsequent heavy rain resulting in the infamous flood of 1952.

A lot of shells were fired across the moor and the Royal Engineers were tasked with clearing them after the war, but according to one local, sometimes they just buried them and carried on!

So, overall, Exmoor is a wonderful place to walk but take care. When we first came here to live, we were told that you are never in fact far from civilisation but that it feels far more remote than you might think at first glance of an O.S. map.

Ref: The field archaeology of Exmoor. Hazel Ridley and Robert Wilson-North
ISBN 1 873592 58 2

9

Brendon Common

Helen's Tale

This was going to hurt. Tess had no time to brace herself before she hit the top pole with her left hip. The remaining three poles collapsed beneath her as she landed in an awkward heap. The ground rushed up to meet her head. Dazed for a moment, she righted her horizon from the uncomfortable position she had landed in and looked around.

Balthazar, her horse stood on the other side of the pole pile, swivelling his ears seemingly with an expression of disappointment that she hadn't actually cleared the jump.

Upon hauling herself up, the pain hit her. Her left hipbone throbbed, her right shin hurt where it had bashed a pole and her shoulder felt as though it had been jarred in its socket. She could hear Jean's voice in the back of her head now, a stout ruddy faced woman who always wore a headscarf, 'if you don't require an ambulance, you're getting back up!'

'Sod that,' thought Tess picking herself up from the grass, 'not today.'

She gingerly limped around the broken jump and grabbed Balthazar's reins. He followed her with his long dark face, ears still swivelling. She felt Balthazar lose his pace after the third jump and the normally long loping horse decided to shorten his stride and pull up before the fourth. Tess however, had kept on going.

As she hobbled along, pulling Balthazar towards the exit, Jean approached her.

'You could have carried on, you know. You only had four faults.'

Tess shook her head.

'It's not worth it. There's already six clear rounds. Besides, Balt did the same thing yesterday in practice, but I felt him shorten as we landed and we didn't take the jump.' 'That's a shame. I was crossing everything for you to go clear. Violet's up next. Maybe she can do it. We've still got a chance to take the cup.'

'I know but I need to get Balt checked out. Maybe he's lame.'

Jean's expression hardened.

'He looks fine to me.'

Tess shrugged and made her way to the horse boxes with Balthazar in tow. She found their trailer and tied him up. Balt tugged at the hay net hanging on the side and stood munching innocently.

'Maybe next year eh, Balt?' Tess removed her helmet and loosened the girth. It was a shame she had let her team down. They were a dead cert for the trophy but it would probably go to a Somerset team. It would have been nice to keep the prize in Devon for one more year.

Tess held Balthazar as he stood patiently in the yard while the vet ran her hands down each of his legs. She got Tess to trot him round, checked his hooves, teeth, eyes, as much as she could but couldn't find anything wrong with him. Tess was still convinced there was something amiss, something the vet hadn't found in just a quick half hour visit. Jean told her she was imagining things and needed to be firmer with Balt so he wouldn't get his own way. Tess's boyfriend didn't possess an opinion and tried to stay away from horses because according to him 'one end bites and the other end kicks.'

A few days later, Tess and Jean with Violet and Beth, a stable hand, went out for an early morning hack on over Brendon Common. Jean led the group on her skewbald mare. Violet and Beth rode two of the farm's liveried horses and Tess was on Balthazar. Their usual route took them up the sheep field opposite the stables which opened onto the edge of the moor through a line of gnarled beech trees marking the boundary between the moorland and pasture. When they reached top of the hill, the tracks and trails which zigzagged their way across Exmoor came into view.

The Common stretched out before them, meeting the blue of the horizon with nothing else in sight apart from the scrub of the moorland grasses and a lone red kite shrieking as it circled on the thermals.

Turning left, one of the well-used bridle trails climbed a gradual slope for half a mile towards a viewpoint marked with an ordnance survey marker. The view opened up to encompass a sweeping panorama of Exmoor towards Dunkery Beacon and Somerset. To the far left was the Bristol Channel. The Welsh coast appeared so close Tess felt she could ripple the water surface with her fingertips or simply ride across it.

Jean took the path straight ahead with her mare in a brisk walk, head nodding up and down. This route took them across the higher part of the moor running parallel with the road which cut across the Common effectively dissecting it in two. Violet and Beth followed behind at a lively pace with Balthazar behind.

Beyond the road on the lower part of the Common, Tess made out the red brown haze of a red deer herd, mostly hinds and youngsters. She looked more closely while Balt plodded along, trying to see if she could spot a stag amongst the group with his handlebar antlers, but she was out of luck today. He wasn't there.

A little further on they reached the point where the bridle track crossed a well-trodden trail used by many walkers, horse riders and Land Rovers. This trail carried on in a westerly direction down the moorland valley towards the small hamlet of Malmsmead in the Doone Valley.

Jean, twisted round in her saddle.

'Let's go over to the monument.'

Jean's mare leapt into a brisk canter and the two liveried horses followed her action, not wanting to be left behind. Balthazar made a valiant effort to begin with but despite Tess's efforts to keep him going, she felt his pace slow, and the space between them and the other horses grew wider. Their tails flicked and clods of earth flew as they galloped further into the distance.

'Come on, keep up,' Jean hollered behind her above the sound of the thundering hooves. 'We're nearly there.'

The monument stood alone towards the end of the common, half a mile from the Somerset border. A lonely memorial to a brave army soldier who had served in both World Wars. Made of solid granite approximately five feet tall it bore the words:

IN
MEMORY OF
Colonel R H MACLAREN O.B.E.
M C COMMANDER C W TROOPS
ROYAL ENGINEER WHO WAS
KILLED ON DUTY ON THIS SPOT
MAY 20th 1941.
THIS STONE WAS ERECTED
BY HIS BROTHER OFFICERS.

Jean, being the first one there circled the monument several times while the others caught up. Her mare had stopped and stood snorting indignantly by the time Tess reached them at a slow trot. Balthazar stopped abruptly with the stone level by his left shoulder.

    Jean glared disapprovingly at them.

    'What a silly place to put a lump of rock. It sort of spoils the scenery somewhat,' said Violet.

    'I think it's beautiful,' replied Beth.

    Tess was puzzled.

    'Who was he anyway and how was he killed?'

    'According to local history,' began Jean, 'he was part of a secret rocket testing station during World War II. Something went wrong one day when testing right here in this spot. Colonel whatever-he's-called threw himself on a rocket to stop it injuring the rest of his troop. Others say it was a just a bit of metal that flew out and pierced him in the chest, but that tale's not nearly as dramatic though.'

    'Sounds very heroic to me,' decided Tess.

    'What an amazing place to be buried,' continued Beth.

'No, no, he's buried somewhere in Wiltshire, not here. He only died here,' Jean corrected.

'Ew do you think his ghost is here, roaming across the moors? I heard that parts of Exmoor are haunted. All those creepy little cottages,' Violet smirked, asking her horse to trot. She circled around then headed off back down the moor.

'What nonsense!' snorted Jean. 'Let's be getting back. I've got a new trailer being delivered at 9 o'clock.'

She trotted off with Beth following. Tess asked Balt to move. Nothing happened apart from a nonchalant ear swivel.

'Come on, Balt.'

Still nothing.

She asked him again. His hooves were rooted to the spot. She tried once more, opening the reins at the same time to turn him round but this only resulted in a steep neck bend and no leg movement. Tess looked behind her. The others were way down the moor, almost over the hill and out of sight. She asked him again deepening her voice, hoping he would pick up on the sternness of it.

'Balt. Come on.'

He remained stock still with his shoulder to the monument. Why couldn't they have waited for her? They would have seen that Balt was being stubborn and come back to help. She tried to turn him left around the monument but again his head only turned so it was almost touching the stone. She shortened the reins and became firmer in her request for movement but Balt's head only raised. He didn't even chew the bit or make any normal horse movements. No swishing of his tail, no adjusting his legs, no tossing his head, no reaching forward to chew at the scrub grass. Nothing. He looked straight forward with the occasional swivel of his ears. This was really unusual, but after his dire performance at the show the other day and now this, Tess was convinced the vet must have missed something. She made a mental note to call her again when she got back to the farm.

But the problem now was how to get Balt moving. Maybe he wants a rest, she thought. She waited a few minutes then tried asking and talking to him again but nothing seemed to work. She waited. She dismounted and tried leading. Nothing. She got back on him and waited again. A buzzard circled this time. A couple of cars made their way along the moorland road and grated across the cattle grid at the boundary fence. Clouds swept across the endless horizon. Balt's ears swivelled at every little rustle but he didn't move even one hoof.

'What took you so long?' laughed Violet as Tess led Balt into the stable block. Violet was grooming her bay cob William whom she had ridden at the show. Tess had been slightly envious when Violet had taken the fastest clear round on a horse not nearly as agile as Balt, who being part thoroughbred used to frequently take first place in the team. But that was back in the good old days . . .

'Don't ask,' grumbled Tess, holding back the lump in her throat. 'I missed lunch with my boyfriend and now I'm going to be late for picking up my mum. Can I borrow your phone please?'

'Aw sorry battery's flat.' Violet brushed a sweeping arc across William's flank. 'Anyway I saw you both still standing there when we drove down to Simonsbath a couple of hours ago. Jean was hoping you were going to go with her to see the site for the next show. But you weren't here so I had to go instead.'

Tess led Balt into a stall and took off his saddle.

'I was going with her but I can't just leave Balt in the middle of the moor, can I?' She turned to the wall not letting Violet see her eyes brimming with tears.

'What made him stop?'

'I have no idea. Jean says he's fine. The vet says he's fine. He's not injured from jumping. I got off him and tried to lead him but he wouldn't budge. A friendly hiker tried to lead him but Balt ignored him too. There was nobody else on the moor at all so you can't say he was scared. No low flying planes, no quad bikes. Nothing.'

Violet slid her hand down William's near front leg and started picking his hoof.

'So how did you get him back?'

'I didn't. He just turned around and started walking and I hadn't even asked him to. Walked calmly all the way back here. I was so relieved.'

'Hmm I don't think you're firm enough with him. I can tell you now, there's absolutely no way I would put up with any of that nonsense from Will. He would be off down that moor like a shot because he knows what's good for him.'

Tess sighed and haltered Balthazar, leading out of the stable block and down the path to turn him out into the field. Beth came running up from the farmhouse as she saw them.

'Hi Tess, so glad you got back. Do you know what time it is? Are you both okay?'

'Yeah we're both fine.'

'Great, I am so glad. I can't stop, I gotta take a beginner's ride out at 3 o'clock. But there was a man on the phone about an hour ago worried about you, I guess it was your boyfriend but I told him you'd be back soon. Think he's going to call again shortly. Anyway, just after he phoned, some old man stopped by with this message for you. Don't know who he was but he said he'd seen you both standing by the monument, so I knew you were okay and you'd be back soon.'

'Oh really? Who was it?'

'I don't know. Some really old guy in a beat up Land Rover. But he left you his address and said he could help you and Balt. I dunno, I guess it wouldn't hurt to go see him.'

Beth handed a scrunched up bit of paper from her jodhpur pocket and thrust it into Tess's hand before running off into the stable block.

'I gotta go now, bye.'

'But who was he?' Tess called after her. It all sounded a bit strange.

She looked at the paper. Scrawled on it in pencil was the name of a cottage she didn't recognise in Brendon but no phone number. There was no way her boyfriend would be happy about her going to see a man who she didn't know on the middle of Exmoor. But Tess was desperate. She couldn't bear the thought of selling Balthazar so she had made up her mind. It was a chance she was willing to take.

Tess knocked six times on the weathered oak door. It creaked open. An elderly man stood there in a thick felted cardigan, with a waistcoat underneath. His grey wiry hair stuck out from the sides of his head in wisps. His brown trousers were held around his waist with baling twine.

'Oh hello, I hope you don't mind me calling but my friend said you saw me on the moor the other day and said you might be able to help me and my horse. Do you think you could have a look at him? He hasn't been behaving like himself recently and I need to know what's wrong with him.'

His amber eyes creased into a kindly smile.

'Ah yes. Come in dear and take a seat.'

Tess adjusted her eyes to the low light inside the cottage. The ceilings were low too, supported by dark thick beams. A small fire glowed and crackled in the fireplace, above which was another dark beam as a mantelpiece. A large red deer antler rested on a couple of nails above the mantel. Beneath the antler was a small sepia photograph of a soldier. Tess sighed then dropped onto the nearest armchair, a large, weathered leather monstrosity which looked as though it could tell a few stories, had it miraculously had the ability to speak.

'Now tell me 'bout your 'orse. What's wrong with 'im?'

'Well, he just won't do anything. He's a capable horse, well he was for a while when I first got him. Then he slowly started to seize up and become less accommodating. He's never nasty, always gentle natured. Just the other day, at the show, we had a great start and he threw me at the fourth fence because he didn't want to jump it. And before that, he stopped on a hack. We'd gone a few miles out of the stable onto the Common. I thought I had him under control, we were going well and then he suddenly stopped and didn't want to move. The others went back without us. I was so worried we were going to be stranded on the moor. That must have been when you saw us. By the monument. Took me hours to get him back to the stable. He's just outside if you'd like to have a look at him.'

'Oh no dear, that won't be necessary.' He furrowed his bushy eyebrows. 'Hmmm. Maybe we can fix his remotely? Sometimes the most simple things are the most often overlooked.'

'What do you mean?'

Tess was puzzled. Why didn't he want to look at Balt? Something told her there was no way he was going to leave the confines of his cottage.

'What you need, my dear, is an elixir.'

Tess wasn't sure what he meant.

'To loosen your 'ands my dear. No point havin' you orderin' 'im around and clingin' on for dear life. You 'ave more control when you let go.'

This sounded stupid to Tess. It was the horse who needed help, not her. There was no question of loosening her grip with a horse like Balt. He'd probably have her over more fences that she could count.

He turned and hobbled into his kitchenette. She shifted uncomfortably on the large worn leather chair. Now and then he came into view with two thick grey earthenware mugs in his hand. He set them down on the countertop, poured hot water into them from an ornate copper kettle and came back into the room.

Reaching over the fire he took down the antler from the wall above the fireplace. With the antler in one hand he went over to a large bureau behind Tess's chair and pulled open a drawer.

'Now where did I put it?'

More rummaging, metallic sounds.

'Oh yes, I'll have that.'

Tess noticed a crumpled paper bag he dumped unceremoniously on the bureau top.

More rummaging.

'Haha yer 'tis.'

He went back into the kitchen, antler in one hand and the paper bag and what looked like a wooden handled grater in the other. The antler and grater clattered down on the countertop. His hand reached inside the paper bag and Tess was unable to make out what was in there. It worried her slightly, but this man was her last chance to heal the relationship between her horse and herself so she waited and observed. He scrunched up the object in his hand and sprinkled a little over each of the mugs. What he did next was more alarming.

Grasping the antler in his left hand, and grabbing the grater in the other, he worked the tool on the tip of the longest antler point. White dust showered the mugs and the worktop. When he had finished he swept the dust from the countertop into his palm and sprinkled it evenly between the two mugs. To finish off he grabbed a wooden handled dish mop and stirred both drinks with the handle end of it.

Tess grimaced inwardly, hoping it didn't show on her face. She didn't want to offend the old man who had obligingly agreed to help her. He padded back and handed her one of the mugs. It was warm and the liquid inside was as grey as the mug. Pale creamy-coloured objects of indiscernible origin floated on the top along with the antler dust which hadn't submerged. A herby aroma enveloped her and Tess felt her throat constrict at the thought of drinking it.

He stood in front of her.

'Take a sip, my dear. Won't do you no 'arm.'

She tipped the mug, clenching her nostrils and trying to limit her sense of smell. She felt gentle pressure on the bottom of the mug and had no choice but to take a bigger mouthful than she'd anticipated. It tasted better than it smelt, a little watery like a weak vegetable broth.

Satisfied that she'd taken a mouthful, he sat down on a velvet covered dining chair and drank his own concoction.

Tess pulled the cottage door closed behind her. The light was fading but it should be hours from darkness. She could have sworn that she hadn't spent very long in the old man's cottage, half an hour tops. They hadn't spoken about very much but now dusk crept across the sky. Mounting Balthazar, the sudden upward movement made her feel light-headed, but she urged him into a trot and they headed up the lane towards the main road. Upon nearing the entrance to the stables, something made her turn Balthazar left through the lower field gate and head towards the common.

Maybe it was the disbelief that he had actually been kind and friendly that made her want to ride out to the monument where Balt had stopped and refused to go any further

Maybe it was out of curiosity that some strange soup concoction could actually work.

Balthazar seemed happy enough pacing up the hillside, ears pricked forward. Tess was urging him on, clutching the reins, hoping that he wouldn't stop. At the top of the hill the moor opened out into the familiar dirt track. Balthazar's steady hoof beats took them towards the narrowing pink horizon, away from the sun setting over the ocean.

Tess's head felt suddenly heavy, a tingling sensation crept into her hands and her body felt leaden. She wanted to turn him around but her mind couldn't summon up movement for her body to follow. She tried to grip the reins to pull him up but her will had the opposite effect. Try as she might, her fingers felt like they weren't connected to her wrists and the reins slipped in her grasp. Balt kept plodding on with long strides under the darkening sky. His pace quickened into an easy trot. The track widened. Balt leapt into a canter. Tess tried to regain the reins, which again slipped through her fingers. She shivered upon seeing the mist hanging in strange clumps in the valley down to the left.

As they travelled along the track, the mist swirled along the lower edge in time with Balt's hoof beats. Vague shapes appeared, coming closer with every stride, pulsing with energy in time with Balt's galloping. A large, low hanging mist cloud, growing more and more opaque was travelling fast alongside. As Balt galloped faster, the shape matched his speed, gradually changing into that of a running animal, but it wasn't a real animal, was it?

Tess peered through the falling light at more shapes slowly cementing their form. The largest shape materialised into a majestic deer stag glowing in the dusk, shifting from pearly white to opaque silvery grey and back again, leaping over bushes, ruts, ditches as they travelled further up the track. More animals came into view, several hinds were following the stag. Some formed stouter bodies of the ponies that ran free on the moor and all of them were running alongside.

And Balthazar was running like he had remembered how to be a horse. He ran on and on and on. The monument came into view on the horizon. A dark monolith standing sentinel over the ancient moor. At the monument stone Tess willed her hands to work, finally managing to move them a fraction to the left. Balthazar slowed and circled anti-clockwise in a smooth arc. The animals circled with him, bouncing over tussocks and grass clumps. The same thing happened when they changed direction. Balt spun on his heels, snorted and cantered around the standing stone, his agility returning as he leapt playfully over a tussock before heading back towards the farm at gentle trot.

Tess felt a tingling in her hands and leaden in her legs, squinting through the darkness as the stag bucked and leapt in response as all the animals circled around them, pulsing and glowing, appearing and fading circling and circling until they gradually disappeared into the silent Exmoor landscape.

10

A Man with Antlers

Stephany's Tale

It was a long hard winter, our first year on top of the moor. Finding a place with enough open space to run our riding holidays had been a challenge. We'd been looking for three years, searching across the whole of Exmoor, trying to find somewhere suitable and affordable, a big ask. We had found the most wonderful places only to find they were out of the budget the bank would allow us. We'd put offers on places, only for someone to top them and leave us once again looking. We were almost despairing and on the point of giving up and trying to find a home in Wales, when our new home presented itself. In a lot of ways, it was perfect, on the edge of the moor with a wonderful sea view, miles of open country, a big house, nice fields, lots of stables and outbuildings. We felt that we were lucky to find this place, even though it was high, exposed and on the wettest part of Exmoor. It had a big downside though. It was an uncared for wreak and needed a huge amount of work both inside and out.

Still, we were young and optimistic enough to believe we could do the work needed. We spent the autumn and most of the winter learning new skills to renovate the house, build new stables, fence the fields, put water in the stables and fields and getting rid of the huge amount of rubbish the old owners had left behind. We had help with the most difficult building work and the guys working for us encouraged our efforts, made good our mistakes and worked hard to get everything done as quickly as possible. At last, we could bring the horse over from their grass keep and settle them in. They took to their new home as if they had always been there. The new place began to feel like home rather than a reckless venture.

The cold weather had crept up on us almost unnoticed at first. We'd had weeks of cold strong winds and sideways rain. The horses were determined to stay in their cosy new stables and took a dim view of being exercised in a howling gale. We would have liked to explore the moor, but the weather was against us, so we trotted down the road, past the garage, up another road and home along the track. The moor remained mysteriously clad in mist and unexplored. Our days passed by in a haze of mucking out, painting the rooms in the house, riding head down in the rain and falling knackered into our beds late at night. Occasionally we escaped to town for a day to shop and have a coffee, but that would leave us tucking the horses into bed in the dark and feeling a bit guilty about the work we hadn't finished.

Slowly though we were making progress. Some of the bedrooms were looking good and we moved the furniture stored in the barns into them. We felt hopeful that we would be ready for the first guests by Easter. The first hard frost scuppered our plans though. The water to the house, and worse, to the stable, froze. Thawing enough water every day for the horses and us soon became a long difficult task, taking up most of the day, leaving us cold, wet and angry. There was a lot of bad language. Showering, even washing became a thing of the past as the drainpipes froze and the water in the sinks had to be baled out by hand. We wondered how long it could go on. Then the snow came, at first falling gently, slowly covering everything, deeper and deeper, softening the landscape and so beautiful we were stunned by it. The frost sparkled blue on the flakes, the snow lay like a gentle covering. We were enchanted. But the wind changed all that. Whipping the snow into huge drifts in front of the kitchen door, the stable door, everywhere we needed to get to. We dug ourselves out, laid grit on the paths, tried to make the best of it, but the weather laughed at us. More snow, more wind. At first the beauty and excitement of the snow had thrilled us, but the reality of digging ourselves out and thawing enough water every day for the horses and ourselves soon became a hardship. Soon we were snowed in, nothing could get in or out for weeks and life became a little scary. Sliding down the steep hill on foot to get food was a fun adventure. Trying to get back up again weighed down with essentials was a challenge. On the better days when the ground wasn't so bad we rode the horses down, we could get more essentials and the journey was easier with their help. When the frost hardened, and the ground became rutted and slippery we didn't dare risk them. Our lovely neighbour drove across the fields with desperately needed hay for the horses. 'I've not seen anything like this since 45,' he said. 'The army had to drop hay on the moor for stock then, if this carries on they will have to do it again.' We shuddered at the thought.

Suddenly the weather relented, changing from sparkling ice to muddy slush in a day. It rained and rained and rained. A strong cold wind blew the rain viciously sideways. The horses released from weeks of tottering over frozen fields and walking quietly in hand, churned the fields to a muddy mess. It was hard to believe it was spring. Our hardy neighbours laughed at the woosy southerners. 'You'll have to get used to this, its nine months of winter and three months of bad weather, all part of the land.'

In the midst of this our first guests arrived. We hoped the weather would improve with the spring, but it didn't. Week after week of trying to find safe places for a gallop, wet coats round the aga, soggy horses, soggy tack, soggy guests, soggy us. The guests were cheerful, but I began to wonder if setting up riding holidays on the wettest part of Exmoor had been a bad decision.

'Never seen a spring like it' said our neighbour when we met him moving cattle across the moor in a howling gale. For a moment the whole ride was engulfed by his chunky red cattle, steaming so much in the rain they created their own fog. They were very reluctant to face the weather and we joined in to help, turning the reluctant animals toward the gate and home. When they realised where they were going the whole herd took off in a mad rush, making the horses start and shy. Trying to make sure nobody fell off I barely heard his warning. 'Don't you ever be tempted to go down the B...... water combe to get out of the wind, it belongs to the old ones.' 'Pardon what did you say?' I shouted after him, but he was gone chasing after the cattle.

The wet weather continued, through April and May, spring seemed a distant dream. But finally, finally, the grass started to grow, the horses could be turned out and suddenly it seemed, it was June, nearly halfway through the year. 'At long last the weather relented. Exmoor showed its softer side. The rain stopped, the sun came out and even the wind dropped a bit. We had a few days without guests. After the months of work, we were thrilled to have a few days of freedom. The moor beckoned. Its high hills, its hidden valleys, all unknown to us. Keen to make the most of it we decided to do a long ride, to go further than we had before and to see if we could make a new ride for the guests. It would be good if we could find a new ride. We hadn't had much time to explore since we'd moved and although we knew the moor a little, we'd kept to the tracks and places we already knew.

We picked the best day of the week, got up early, made ourselves a packed lunch and went out to catch our favourite horses. 'Tabu' my jet black lady, her father a Portuguese bull fighting horse and her mother a Dales from the fells of the north. She was clever, sure footed, brave and keen. I'd bred her myself, had ridden her mother for years over Bodmin moor, chosen her sire carefully and we'd been together every day since her birth. She was a good moorland horse, able to pick her way through bogs, find her way over rough ground and most importantly could always find her way home if I got lost. She was a keen explorer too, she liked to find new places, especially if she was allowed to taste them as we went along. Amanda brought in her half-sister Kia, bred from the same sire, but her mother had Arab and quarter horse blood. She was fox red, fast and keen, equally good for this type of ride. They were a bit surprised to be led in so early without their companions and not sure at first that they wouldn't rather spend their day idling in the fields. But after they'd has some breakfast been tacked up and we were on the way they perked up and seemed as keen to explore as we were.

At first we made good progress across the landscape we knew. We galloped across Ilkerton common, then slowed down into a steep wooded combe, through a gate and up onto the wild openness of Furzehill common. Another fun gallop with the wind in our hair, shrieking at the top of our voices and urging our keen mounts to go even faster. We knew the way across these commons and the flat top of Cheriton

Ridge, the track across Brendon common and down into Oare, but we hadn't explored any of the hidden valleys between and this was our goal for the day. 'It would be good if we could find a ride through the valley,' I suggested, 'especially if the weather is rough.'

We'd never gone down into the valley before, it was hidden, a fold in the ground that was unseen until you almost fell into it. There was only one place to get across it, the head of the valley where it widened a bit. There didn't seem to be anyway along it but we had time now, the right horses and no guest to look after. We wandered along the top of the valley looking for a way down but there didn't seem to be one. We went back to the crossing but the way along the valley was blocked by a forest of gorse and hawthorn. We could see a tiny sheep track beneath the trees, could we follow it. We started by trying to duck beneath the prickly branches but had to give up and dismount before we'd gone more than a few yards. The path was steep and narrow but eventually the hawthorns thinned and ran out and we could get back in the saddle. We could water from a little stream babbling below us but we could not see it in the bottom of the valley, which lay steeply below us full of bracken, blackthorn and hawthorn. We were still following the little sheep track, not sure if it was worth going on, but the ground was so steep turning would have been difficult and the thought of going back through the hawthorn wasn't good either.

The horses picked their way carefully along the path, the bracken high ether side making it almost seem as though we were swimming through it. The air was hot down here out of the moorland breeze and pungent with the scent of the bracken. The horses were sweating a bit too adding their horsey scent to the air. Somehow the movement and the smells were making us feel slightly dozy and dizzy. It was like being in a different land, the hill stretching high above us covered in bracken and gorse with the occasional hawthorn towering above the thick foliage, strangely the hawthorns were still in bloom and as we rode past their musky perfume would add to the odd toxication we were feeling. 'Much more of this and I'm going to fall asleep and tumble off Tabu' I said. Amanda didn't answer. I turned in the saddle and found her right behind me swaying in her saddle eyes closed. I stopped and Kia bumped into Tabu who raised her leg in warning. Before I could say anything Amanda opened her eyes. 'Oooh I think I dozed off for a second' 'Yeah you did' I agreed. 'It's stifling down here.' We went on trying to be more alert, the little track started to go downhill into the bottom of the valley widening as it went. Here the bracken gave way to short cropped grass and we could see the stream tumbling through rocks at the bottom of the valley.

    Soon we reached the bottom, riding into a little wildflower meadow, ringed with a circle of hawthorns and rowan, ahead of us great mounds of stone and earth covered the side of the hill. We stopped the horses. 'We could have lunch here,' suggested Amanda. We got off and tied the horses loosely to a little rowan tree so they could graze and got out our lunch. We sat looking along the stream at the mounds on the hill. 'They look like troll houses,' I said. Amanda laughed and shook her head. 'Old silver workings more likely. There's a bigger track going up the hill beside them, we could use it to go out.'

I looked round, the ground by the stream was flat and looked safe enough. 'We could follow the stream to the end of the valley and see if we can go back on the other side, look there is another track coming down the other side of the stream, perhaps we could go up that or even further along. Do we have time?'

Amanda looked at her watch. 'It's nearly high noon on the longest day of the year, I'm sure we have time to go anywhere. Isn't it supposed to be some kind of magic day though?' 'No isn't that sometime in May or Halloween?' I replied. 'Who knows? But I feel like a little nap, it's so warm and that stream is making me sleepy.' I laughed Amanda was famous for her "little naps".

She closed her eyes, I looked round, it was the most beautiful place, with the tinkling stream, the pretty meadow, the flowering hawthorns, the bright red berries on the rowan, The bright blue sky above, the warmth of the sun, the lovely wild smell of nature. It was so quiet I could hear the horses chewing the grass above the sound of the stream. I had time to think it a bit odd that there were berries on the rowan, before I too fell asleep. I think only a few seconds passed before something woke me.

The sun was still high in the sky, but something had changed, the valley no longer seemed so welcoming, it was wilder somehow. It felt more like another world as it had when we came down into the valley, but more so now. I felt I had somehow slipped out of my time and place. Amanda was still there asleep in the sun, but the horses had stopped eating, they were alert, tense, looking up at the hill opposite. Tabu snickered, a sound of greeting lowering her head for a second almost as though she was bowing. Kia was more nervous, showing the white round her eyes and shuffling her feet, moving to the end of the rope as though she wanted to break away. Before I could get to my feet to go to her, Tabu nudged her, and she quietened. They both looked up the hill again. I got to my feet.

I saw him then, the great antlers first, a royal, not on the head of a stag but on a man, tall lean, majestic, with his red and white hounds beside him. Coming straight toward me. He didn't seem to notice me. I leant over to Amanda as he came down the hill.

'Wake up, wake up, there's a man coming down the hill with antlers on his head.' As I said it, I realised how silly it sounded. Maybe it was someone in fancy dress but if so it was still a bit weird. Amanda grunted and opened her eyes but didn't seem fully awake. He was getting closer, nearer to the other side of the stream, but ignored us. He nodded to the horses. Kia flared her nostrils and stepped back but Tabu nodded back to him. "What the fu...!' exclaimed Amanda as he crossed the stream and walked past us, dogs milling around him. He walked onto the track by the hillocks and vanished behind them. The world seemed to change, again the tension went from the air, the horses relaxed. We were back in the valley again.

'What did you see,' I asked.

'I don't know: a man with antlers and dogs, a stag being chased by dogs, but it wasn't running.'

'What was he wearing, what did he look like?' I asked again, trying to decide myself what I had really seen.

'I dunno, some kind of fringed buckskin jacket and chaps maybe, but I'm not sure. It could have just been fur, I was dreaming when you woke me, he had wild fierce eyes though not like a normal stag. What did you see?'

'A man with the antlers of a stag, I think, red and white hounds at least eight, but maybe it was a stag, I'm not sure they have horns this time of year, aren't they just growing them?'

'Maybe it was someone in fancy dress! I definitely saw the dogs though, couldn't tell you what breed they were. I've never seen anything like them before, big weren't they?'

'Should we try and follow him, see if we can get a better look?'

Amanda shuddered. 'No, let's go up the path he came down, see if we can see any tracks.'

We led the horses up the path but we saw no tracks, no sign anyone had been there. But I felt we were no longer in the same place or even the same time. We were back in our world now.

We were quiet on the way home. We explored the valley again, we found a lovely route right round the valley, we led the guests through the valley often and we picnicked in the hawthorn meadow with them. But we never saw the hawthorn with flowers and the rowan with berries at the same time again. And although we saw deer in the valley, we never saw them with hounds, and we never again saw one who could have been a man.

11

He Wanted to Try

Anne's Tale

The elderly man walking up the path was slightly stooped but his pace was steady. He had left Lynmouth an hour earlier and was well on his way to his objective which was the Iron Age fort above the beautiful Watersmeet confluence of the east and west Lyn rivers.

He bristled as he remembered the intrusive manner in which he had been served his breakfast at the small hotel. The waitress had been unnecessarily bent on engaging him in conversation until he had finally shared his plans for the day. The wretched woman had then had the temerity to suggest the walk he had in mind was too strenuous for a man of his years! Adding unnecessary advice about how short the autumn days were becoming and that the weather could change suddenly.

He was perfectly capable of making his own decisions and didn't need advice from silly women.

He was also perfectly capable of eating his meals in silence.

He had been doing so for years.

*

As the path became steeper his pace eased slightly and he paused to look around. He could not see very far or very clearly. He knew his sight was failing, and at his most recent hospital appointment had received the news that very little could be done and that it was only a matter of time before he would become blind. He was suffering from the 'wet' form of macular degeneration, the onset had been sudden and perhaps he had been foolish not to go the GP earlier but there was no point crying over spilt milk. The diagnosis neither surprised nor dismayed him. His life was simple, he had always preferred the radio to television and was determined not to let age or infirmity constrict him until it was unavoidable. Hence his trip to North Devon. He had no interest in foreign travel and had not been outside Britain since the war. During the early years of his marriage they had not had the money for holidays, and when their son was little, short trips to small coastal resorts had been the most they managed. He thought briefly of the time they had come to Lynmouth, their son had been a toddler and he had insisted that it was a suitable resort, despite the lack of sandy beaches. He abhorred places like Woolacombe – huge, overcrowded and endless rows of shops selling tat and fish and chips. Helen had been happy to avoid the crowds too and in fact the trip had been going well until... he stopped. No point in raking over something which could not be undone, time to press on to his objective. He shook his head as if to rid himself of unwanted thoughts and resumed his walk, quickening his pace slightly.

Before long the path emerged into a wide open space. On the far side he knew there was a set of steps up a steep ridge but the fort was somewhere to his left. He walked across and tried to get his bearings, remembering now that he had left his guidebook back at the hotel. From memory he knew that there was very little left of the Iron age fort but he wanted to walk round it's edge and imagine. It was not hard to see why this would have been a good site to build and live in. Access to water, shelter, and beautiful- would Iron Age man and woman have appreciated that? He was sure that there was a couple of plaques giving some brief details and marking the site. His tunnel vision made it difficult, but as he leaned in he was sure there was something but too late realised he was losing his balance on the grassy edge. He tried to turn and move back but fell awkwardly. The sound of a bone breaking preceded a shaft of pain and he fainted.

*

He had no idea how long he'd passed out for, probably just a minute or so, but the pain was making him gasp. He took regular deep breaths and felt his heart rate slow a little and he had the ability to think about his situation. It was obvious he could not get onto his feet- the hotel knew where he was going but were unlikely to raise the alarm until the following morning. He was alone, had got himself into a mess and had to endure it. The parallels with so much of his life struck him, particularly his marriage which had also been fractured by events in this place.

*

They had stopped for a snack, sitting on the small blanket he had carried in his backpack. His son sat on his lap whilst Helen unpacked drinks and some fruit and biscuits. He had leant over to pick up an apple and as he did so his jacket fell open and Richard grabbed at the inside and triumphantly got hold of a piece of paper which he waved about. As Peter tried to retrieve it Richard spotted a game and kept waving and giggled excitedly until it flew out of his hand and was picked up by Helen. It was a letter and she saw the first few words 'My darling...' and the date which was two months earlier.

'That is private, give it to me.'
'I'm sure it is, but I have seen it now.'

And so the whole sorry saga had had to be revealed.

*

He was back in South Africa. The heat was extraordinary and his army uniform was thick and scratchy. His unit was on route to Australia and had a few days leave in Cape Town. Most of the men were already in bars getting drunk and trying to chat up local women, but he preferred to be on his own. He sometimes felt he was destined to spend his life not quite fitting in. He had been born in the last days of the First World War, three weeks after his father had been killed in the battle of Amiens. His mother had been stoical but it had rapidly become apparent that living with her parents was not a long term prospect. When Peter was a year old she had started to look for work and answered an advertisement for a live in housekeeper. At the interview she had been honest about her circumstances, expecting the response she was getting used to- a kind, or at times abrupt, rejection.

Henry Stapleton had been different. He had seen both her strength and her tired desperation and instinctively knew she would make the situation work. He offered her the post, she and Peter had moved in within a fortnight, an arrangement that lasted until Stapleton's death 20 years later.

He grew fond of Peter and quietly made enquiries about schools and found a boarding school which offered scholarships to war orphans. His mother had been initially reluctant but came to realise it was an opportunity she would not otherwise ever be able to access for him and so at the age of seven he had left the only home he had known for the unknown of an institution 50 miles away.

He was neither happy nor unhappy there. He didn't make friends but became self-sufficient with his own company. He was neither academically gifted nor a sportsman but coped in class and on the sports field and was never a victim of bullying, his isolation appeared to protect him, and there were other more vulnerable targets to be picked on.

His mother visited once a term, and there were holidays, but by the time he left at 15 the characteristics of staying apart from others and keeping his emotions dampened down were set.

However, he was also diligent and reliable, and these led to a secure but pedestrian job within the lower ranks of the Civil Service.

When war broke out, he didn't volunteer but early in 1940 received his call up papers and viewed this pragmatically.

Once again, he found himself part of an institution where he could, by dint of a well-practiced effort, fit in, without being noticed particularly by either his peers or superiors.

He was therefore wholly unprepared for an encounter in Cape Town with a young shop assistant when he was looking for something he could buy for his mother. Leila was pretty and chatted easily with him, and steered him towards a small brooch which he could not really afford but bought anyway. On an incredible impulse, he asked if he could see her that evening and to his astonishment she agreed.

Peter was overwhelmed by emotions he had never experienced before. The impatience of waiting to see her again, the pain and joy that these meetings evoked.

Over the next few days they met as often as her working hours would permit and to his astonishment Peter found himself able to articulate his feelings which grew by the day.

'I have never felt like this about anyone in my life.'

The last meeting had been both wonderful and painful. He had taken her to an expensive restaurant (again more than he could afford) and afterwards they had walked for an hour, reluctant to separate for what they both knew could be the final time. They had exchanged addresses and kissed, and she had got on her bus and was gone. Peter resumed his guarded persona, returned to his ship, but dared to think about a future which had Leila in it.

They had corresponded for the duration of the war and once demobbed Peter began to plan and to start to describe what they could do. It would involve waiting and saving, both to pay for her passage to Britain, and initially they would have to live with his mother who now had a tenancy of a small, terraced house in Whitstable. Leila's letters began to be less frequent and shorter. In the end a letter arrived ending their relationship. Leila's own background was grindingly poor, and she had allowed herself to think that Peter offered a way out to a different life. She had slowly realised that in fact she would be exchanging one type of poverty for a similar existence halfway across the world. She loved Peter but hated poverty more. A regular client at the shop had begun to show more than just an interest in jewellery and she had encouraged him, and it was becoming obvious that he would offer her materially more than Peter could ever hope to. He was middle aged, overweight and the most she could hope was to feel an affection for him. But he was affluent and offered her a way out of her dreary life which she was determined to take.

All this she told Peter in one devastating letter. He never replied.

Two years later Peter became aware that Helen in the finance department always lingered when returning his work. One day he asked if he could join her table in the canteen. Helen was unlike Leila in every way. Plain, quiet and unlikely to ever evoke the depth of feeling which he had experienced in South Africa. Almost imperceptibly they inched towards a relationship. Peter looked ahead and realised he wanted more than living either with his mother or alone. A year after their first dinner date he proposed and was accepted.

It was helpful to have something to aim for, his work efforts increased, and he achieved a small promotion which involved a move to the Midlands. Property was much cheaper than in the southeast, and by dint of careful saving on Helen's part they were able to buy a small semi-detached house in the suburbs of Wolverhampton and when they had been married three years Richard was born. Peter was satisfied with his life.

Until on a visit to his mother in Kent, she gave him a letter which had arrived for him from South Africa. Leila was a widow, and arriving in the UK for a holiday and wanted to see him.

Once again he was unprepared for the avalanche of emotion which swept over him. Every logical instinct told him to ignore the letter. He managed to convince himself that by arranging to meet he could prove to himself that his feelings for her were now a fantasy to be exposed as such. It was the first deception, which led to replying to her letter and two months later a meeting in London. For the first time in their marriage he lied to Helen, saying he had been sent to

London for a seminar on pending legislative changes which affected his area of work.

So he and Leila had met. She was still astonishingly beautiful and his feelings for her still as unstoppable and overwhelming. For most of the day he allowed himself to block out the rest of his life and pretend that it was right to be with the woman he loved. Eventually he told the truth, that he was married with a young son. Her face showed shock, then pain then fury.

'Then why are you here?'

He was silent. Impossible to explain or do anything other than leave.

'I'm sorry,' and he walked away and did not look back.

So now the whole story had to be revealed. After Richard was asleep, Helen listened in stony silence to the whole history. At one point he made a half-hearted attempt to defend himself

'I will never see her again, I only... we never...'

'How dare you, you have lied and deceived me in more ways than I can say. I am your wife, and I will continue to live with you and we have a son to raise. But I will never forgive you.'

And in his heart he knew the greatest betrayal had been to love, and still love, Leila.

And so their lives had continued. Helen was meticulous in providing the material needs of a home but never spoke to him beyond the purely functional. She was wholly devoted to Richard who in turn sensing something, progressively detached himself from his father and focussed on his mother.
All communication was purely functional.
'I am out this evening playing bridge.'
'I am taking Richard to see my parents at the weekend.'
In turn he had returned to the lifestyle with which he had been for so long been accustomed, being alone.

Once Richard had left home the house became a silent tomb for both of them. Helen absented herself as much as she could, leaving plates of food to be warmed over a pan of hot water.

Shortly after his retirement she began to show signs of ill health, which was eventually diagnosed, too late, as cancer. She chose to stay in hospital at the end, with Richard by her side.

That was ten years ago now, and as he lay in undergrowth he reflected on how the habits of a lifetime had prevented him from making relationships with anyone subsequently, even his son.

Richard was punctilious in remembering his birthday and at Christmas invited him to stay which he always refused. Once again he was neither happy nor unhappy but filled his day with the radio and reading.

*

He was starting to shiver and feel constantly slightly sick and lightheaded. The pain was persistent but by dint of not moving he at least was not aggravating it further. He was contemplating how this was a particularly stupid way to die and the irony of it happening in the place where so much of his life had begun to unravel. There no longer seemed any point in avoiding reflection on what a failure he had been in so many ways, when suddenly a large dog appeared, sniffing, and then startled to see him. Mustering all his strength he shouted for help, which luckily triggered the dog into a flurry of barking.

'Sadie, Sadie! What have you found?'

'Good god!'

The next couple of hours were a blur but the relief of knowing he was found, would be taken to hospital and would in all likelihood not die, was overwhelming. The pain relief administered by the paramedics had been blissful. The crisp efficiency of the hospital staff reassuring.

'Do you want anyone notifying?'

His immediate reaction was to say no, but instead he heard himself giving Richard's name and telephone number. He wanted to see him. He wanted to see if he could break the habits of a lifetime. Perhaps it was not too late for him to build a relationship with his son.

He knew he wanted to try.

And so, they were done.
Their tales were told.
The air had warmed, and where there had been snow, there was now a steady fall of rain.
The members of the book club filed out into the slushy darkness.
'Golly, that was revealing.'
'Who'd have thought.'
'Well I never did.'
'Phew, what next?'

The Lynton Library Book Club has 15 members. The club meets once a month, in people's homes, or in local pubs, to discuss a book supplied by the Exeter Lending Library. The title is selected by the lending service from a list of 400 titles. Sometimes the members receive a book they have requested, at other times unrequested books have proved to be a surprising delight. In addition to the book supplied by the lending service, the club members take it in turns to nominate a Classic, which is discussed bi-monthly. Having wide-ranging tastes, members also use the opportunity of the meeting to present other books they are reading.

During the pandemic, the group formed The Pandemic Poets Society, and through zoom meetings, they composed and subsequently published a book of poems to which every member contributed, each poem describing and recording the stage the pandemic had reached: our response to the NHS, our thoughts on politicians, our view of lockdowns. Telling Tales is the groups second publishing endeavour.

In addition to books, there is cake, company and camaraderie.

The current members are...

Helen Bolton
Maria Floyd
Carolynn Gold
Lesley Goodman
Auriel Hill
Clair Hughes
Marthe Kiley-Worthington
Anne King
Graham Lavender
Jill Moore
Angie Percival
Stephany Pettinger
Sharon Plant
Chris Sleep
Pat Young

Lynton Library
We are indebted to the staff of Lynton Library for their support and forbearance; we have a tragic reputation for returning books late, which holds up the lending process for the scheme, but we endeavour to improve, while hiding behind the excuse that it is because we cannot bear to part with some books. No? Won't wash? Our hugely humble apologies, you lovely people you.

Printed in Great Britain
by Amazon